Anonymous

The Revolutionary Tendencies of the Age

their cause and their ultimate aim

Anonymous

The Revolutionary Tendencies of the Age
their cause and their ultimate aim

ISBN/EAN: 9783337235352

Printed in Europe, USA, Canada, Australia, Japan

Cover: Foto ©Andreas Hilbeck / pixelio.de

More available books at **www.hansebooks.com**

THE REVOLUTIONARY TENDENCIES OF THE AGE

THEIR CAUSE AND THEIR ULTIMATE AIM

G. P. PUTNAM'S SONS

NEW YORK
27 West Twenty-third Street

LONDON
24 Bedford Street, Strand

The Knickerbocker Press

1897

The Knickerbocker Press, New York

CONTENTS.

THE REVOLUTIONARY TENDENCIES OF THE AGE:

THEIR CAUSE AND THEIR ULTIMATE AIM.

CHAPTER I.

INTRODUCTION.

IN the midst of the blue waters of a distant sea, lies an island of wondrous beauty. Rising gradually from the shores are hills, and back of these are mountains which pierce the sky.

So long had the good people who dwelt on this island lived as they now lived; so fixed were their thoughts and customs, that they learned to look on the laws which governed them as part of the eternal and immutable system of the universe. Thus, while many were familiar with discomfort, and suffered at times great misery, it occurred to but few that their unenviable existence was the result of human regulations; and that a change in these might improve their condition. How, they asked themselves, could they alter that which had always existed—yes, as far back as the memory of man could extend? In winter, with ice on the waters and snow on the fields, the sun gave less warmth than their shivering bodies desired. Could they remedy this? The sun was so distant were it not useless to complain?

And the people kept on in their way—the same old way—thinking it was the only way. They wondered at nothing. A stranger, however, coming from a far-a-way land, and wandering over the island in search of information, wondered at many things he saw. Wherever he travelled, he observed that the same conditions prevailed: the picturesque hills and fertile valleys were reserved for a few manors, while the unattractive plains were covered with huts, built closely together. These had no verdure around them; nay, no more land than was required for them to stand on.

Prompted by curiosity, the stranger inquired at many of the humble doors why, for no apparent reason, so noticeable a difference existed between the habitations of men who were all of the same race. But he inquired in vain.

Leaving the plains, he strolled up the hillsides, among the terraced gardens, the flowers of which filled the atmosphere with fragrance. Between the groves of trees he espied lakes over whose crystal expanse sailed pleasure boats wafted by the breezes from the eastern seas. In the centre of lawns played fountains whose waters, shooting heavenward, fell like myriad brilliants scattered in the sun. Birds of rich and varied plumage were attracted to the spot; and while some flitted in the air to catch the refreshing spray, others, hidden in the foliage, sent forth melodious notes to express their joy of living. Wise birds—and more fortunate than many islanders—to choose such abodes!

Approaching the summit of a mountain, the wanderer saw, seated on a rock, a hermit, lost in meditation.

"Forgive me, good hermit, for disturbing your thoughts. I am a stranger in these parts, and would fain learn from you why it is the manor-houses, few in number, are surrounded by abundant verdure, while the huts, too numerous to count, have not a plot of grass."

"You disturb not my thoughts, O stranger; mine travel the same path as yours. The hut-dwellers have no verdure because they own no portion of this island whereon to cultivate it. Even were they lords of many fields, of what avail would these be without water to make them fertile?"

"And have they not water sufficient to irrigate land?"

"Alas!" exclaimed the hermit, "they deem themselves fortunate in securing enough wherewith to quench their thirst. Think not, however, that water is scarce. From time immemorial it has been flowing, in generous streams, from the mountains into the valleys; yet the plains of the hut-dwellers are arid."

"And why is this thus?" inquired the stranger.

The hermit's eyes flashed as, rising from the rock, he pointed his withered hand to the regions beneath: "Ask the greed of the few; ask the folly of the many! I, years ago, saw the iniquity of that which now causes you to wonder. I proclaimed it to all who would listen, and urged them to action; but the untutored people failed to grasp the meaning of my words; and the lords of the manors, alarmed at my doctrines, exiled me to the forest and the mountain, as a wild beast, dangerous to human life."

Taking his companion by the hand, the hermit led him to a point from which they could dis-cern, in the distance, a mighty cataract dashing over rocks into a lake below. The cataract was unapproachable, and the lake, surrounded by a massive wall, was closely guarded.

"See, O stranger, that bountiful supply of crys-tal water, springing from the breast of Mother Earth. Yet you and I, her thirsting child-ren, cannot wet our lips therewith. Observe those conduits of solid metal, winding like paths down the mountain side. Each one empties in a reservoir attached to the various manors. It is this delicious water which irrigates the fields and gardens, and brings forth the luxuriant verdure which charms the eye, the luscious fruit which delights the palate, the vines from which are pressed the wines which stimulate fancy. It is the elixir of life. And the lords have a mono-poly thereof. They allot to the hut-dwellers, who are their slaves, sufficient to keep them alive, and no more, and this is given them, not as their right, nor yet in a spirit of benevolence, but that they may retain strength to do the work of the morrow. Those who toil not must thirst. Thirst is quenched only in exchange for labor performed ; hence those who are unable to find a master willing to buy their labor, must beg of their neighbors or die. And this, mark you, when an abundance of the life-sustaining fluid is made to supply lakes for pleasure boats to sail on, and fountains for birds to flutter in."

"This is indeed strange," said the wanderer.

"Yet you know not half the strangeness thereof," replied the hermit. "Consider that notwithstanding this plenty, this superabundance, many of those who enjoy it are constantly accumulating, constantly striving for more. Not only do they restrict to a minimum the allowance of those whose labor and assistance are essential to them—of those who built, maintain and guard the wall around the lake, the conduits leading therefrom, and the reservoirs into which they empty—but they combine, and scheme, and resort to innumerable, and often questionable, methods to draw from their neighbors' supply, and thus increase their own."

"What—having more than they require, their greed instigates them to draw from others?"

"Ah—that were little harm if, after surfeiting themselves; if, after satisfying the wants of their steeds and their hounds, they permitted the surplus, the overflow, to run where it should naturally gravitate—to the thirsting toilers be-low; if they allowed them a little verdure, a few flowers, and the joy that these bring."

"How many are there who dwell in the manor-houses?" asked the stranger.

"A thousand."

"And how many in the huts?"

"A million."

"A million fools!"

"You re-echo my words," exclaimed the her-mit exultingly. Then, in tones wherein hope blended with sorrow, he continued:

"Many weary years have elapsed since I told them of their folly; but, alas! I was one of them —a poor prophet in his own poor land. Go you, O stranger, and speak to them. They may listen to your voice, for I have heard it said new lights have come to them of late. Ask them, the children of this luxuriant isle, why they thirst when the mountains are belching forth water, and the reservoirs are overflowing; ask them why they allow their toil to prove so fruitful to those who toil not, and so barren to themselves; ask them, and ask them loudly, why they tolerate in some the sin of waste, while others know the bitterness of want. Go,

O stranger, amongst them. Perhaps the soil is more receptive, the seed more ripe. Plant it in their midst. May it grow, may it fructify; may it bring plenty to all men."

CHAPTER II.

A SURVEY OF THE EXISTING STATE OF THINGS, IN
RESPECT TO THE DIVISION OF THE GOOD AND
THE FAIR THINGS OF THIS WORLD.

THE Lord of the Manor is a fortunate
mortal. This earth, a valley of tears to
so many, is to him a charming abode. Indeed,
it would appear as though all that was best and
fairest thereon was created for him, since his
surroundings are the most delightful known,
and the life he leads the most desired by man.
He has more manors than one. Wherever
nature is most attractive, there he casts his tent.
When the cold winds blow, and snow covers
the land, he takes wing for the sunny south,
where the sky is blue and the air is balmy; he
seeks the shade of the palm-tree and the olive,
and he dreams of many things—but not of the
rigors of winter. Ere the heat of summer
comes, he wanders back to his northern home,
to partake of that which the south can no

longer afford—the more exciting life, and the cool, refreshing breezes. Wherever he goes, pleasure attends him, luxury surrounds him. Men, human like himself, follow all his movements and await, with anxious eye, the sign of command to do his bidding; they supply all his wants and relieve him of any task that might require effort or produce fatigue. His home is a palace, rivalling in magnificence that of princes. He points with pride to the tapestried walls and to many works of art, of priceless value, representing the inspirations, also the labors, of the gifted of nature. His halls, ablaze with light, resound with the merry laughter of fair dames and their cavaliers. They eat from golden plates, and drink from crystal goblets, while strains of entrancing music combine with the vapors of wine to give birth to enchantment. Sometimes austere, from surfeit of indulgence, he is more often a prince of good fellows, a scoffer of all that smacks not of merriment, a reveller at the banquet of life, a gambler and a careless loser, a generous and a general lover—taking pleasure in strange adventures, in surpassing romances, in daring, gallant, sometimes conscienceless, intrigues ; and, withal, deeming the earth his play-ground, and

holding in contempt all humanity which is beyond the pale of his own charmed circle.

Here let us pause and reflect.

To live as the Lord of the Manor lives, in
stately style, requires, as is obvious to all, great
riches; for without these, the pleasures and
luxuries he enjoys would be beyond his reach,
as they are beyond the reach of all who are
poor. It is no less obvious that it requires
effort, great effort, to create riches. Certainly
wealth, and that which it affords, cannot spring
from idleness; and the Lord of the Manor is
idle. Yet he has of all things in abundance—
in abundance which leads to satiety.

How does a condition so strange as this
arise? Who is this particular man that he
should occupy a position so exalted, so excep-
tional, so enviable among men? Since wealth
can only be produced by effort, was he once a
mighty worker, now enjoying the fruit of his
labor? Is he a valiant warrior, the hero of
many victories, resting on his laurels? Is he,
by birth or by election, the ruler of his fellows,
and as the representative of these, surrounded
by high state, pomp, and splendor? Is he a
mental prodigy, or a model of physical pro-
portions, to be thus discerned and honored

among the multitudes ? Is he the benefactor of the people, their idol, since they allow him the undisturbed enjoyment of privileges and ad-vantages which are denied the majority of the people ?

No, he is none of these. Observe him well; he is in appearance, in speech, in manner, in knowledge, not unlike a thousand other men who pass by, but dare not enter the manor gates. And yet, though he is neither worker, ruler, nor warrior; neither eminent in mind nor perfect of body ; neither magistrate, philosopher, nor benefactor, he lives as though he were entitled, in his single person, to the dignities, emoluments, and privileges all these combined might be entitled to. He has every advantage conceivable; he enjoys every comfort, every luxury, every pleasure. The roadways of the earth are open to him, and he travels through continents as through his own domains. And wealth, which is the means of securing all this, comes to him without effort, physical or mental, on his part; it comes to him as does the sun-shine to the fields, as does the dew to the flowers.

But does not the golden radiance in which the fields bask ; does not the freshness which the flowers draw from the silvery dew, imply the working of mighty forces in distant spheres beyond? Is there not, somewhere in our solar system—in the very heart thereof—a power which toils to produce that which the fields and the flowers enjoy and profit by without labor or effort on their part? And so likewise, does not the radiance in which the Lord of the Manor lives; do not the splendors and lavishness which surround him, imply the working of mighty forces somewhere? Some, surely, must exert themselves in some quarter or other, to obtain these results, for they cannot be obtained without exertions. Aladdin's lamp does not shine save in the thousand and one nights of the far Eastern skies; the fairy's wand does not gratify extravagant wishes, erect noble castles, and provide sumptuous feasts, by its mere waving in mortal's feeble hand ; nor, however favored the Lord of the Manor may be, does nature, for his benefit, suspend her eternal laws, and produce effect without cause, wealth without labor.

Since, therefore, wealth is only produced and maintained by toil, and since the Lord of the Manor toils not, and yet receives and spends great wealth, there must, of necessity, exist a band of hardy men who exert themselves to produce and maintain this wealth; and yet allow him, fortunate mortal! to reap the main benefits thereof; allow him, while they labor, to spend his days in indolence—sailing over limpid waters, fishing in quiet brooks, hunting in shady forests, travelling through distant lands —eating, drinking, feasting, loving—dreaming not of, caring not for, those who weave for him his purse of Fortunatus.

In this way, and in this way alone, can we account for the otherwise unaccountable fact, that the Lord of the Manor, passing his time in leisure, enjoys those results which, it is claimed, are the fruit of labor.

  *   *   *   *   *

The Lord of the Manor who, in common parlance, is the opulent landowner, is indebted, for the advantages he enjoys, to no ingenious devices. The methods he employs are simple. His land is productive; but he has such vast fields it is quite impossible for him to make them productive by his own efforts; moreover, he has no disposition, and, further still, there is no necessity for him, to do so. Favored among other men in being the possessor of many acres, why should he not be still further favored among them, by not having to submit to the same conditions as they have to submit to—work and worry to live?

In the attainment of this end, circumstances favor him admirably. He and his brother land-owners own so much land, there is little or none left for the remainder of humanity. Men have the desire to live; life, unfortunately, is not self-sustaining; hence, to live, men must culti-vate the soil and draw therefrom the wherewith to sustain life. Herein it is that the Lord of the Manor is master of the situation. The majority of men having no land, and yet being dependent thereon for their maintenance, must do one of two things: either starve or appeal to the owner that his fields may be cultivated to furnish them the necessaries of life. From this there is no escape. Their necessities will com-pel them to appeal to him, and their necessities are his opportunity. He, not unwillingly, grants their request; but on one condition: the culti-vation of the soil shall be considered a privilege, the granting of which shall require that the cultivator of the land surrender to the owner thereof a goodly portion of its produce, or its equivalent.

The privilege of cultivating the soil is not

the only one which the landowner has the power to grant. Men have not wings like the birds; nor have they fins like the fish; hence they cannot soar in the air, nor dwell in the water; but must, perforce, if they live at all, live on the earth—they must occupy space thereon sufficient to hold their bodies. But since they own no portion of this earth, how can they occupy any portion thereof without infringing on the rights of those who own it? Here, once more, the landowner comes to the rescue. He, who owns the land, will provide sufficient for the mass of bodies which are sent to dwell in this world. Not only will he provide the land, but he will draw from the wealth accumulated from the rental of his fields, and he will build houses in the cities; and there will the multitudes find a place of rest, a place of shelter—but always on the same condition as imposed on those who cultivate the soil: the privilege granted must be paid for in the shape of rent.

Thus it is clear that to occupy space on this earth sufficient to domicile the body; to draw from this earth the produce necessary to sustain life, is, to vast numbers, a privilege, not inherent to them as men, as inhabitants of this planet; not dispensed to them by the ruling powers of the universe; not granted to them by the government, the laws of men; but accorded them by certain individual members of the race, who demand, and obtain in exchange therefor, a tribute, known as rent.

Rent, to be paid—and its payment is mandatory—must be earned; to be earned implies labor; and it is for the payment of rent, in its various forms, that multitudes toil. The fruit of this toil constitutes the revenue of the Lord of the Manor; and the extent of this revenue determines the size and the magnificence of his mansions, the number of persons who compose his retinue, the abundance and delicacy of his table, the luxury of his surroundings, the power he controls, the position he occupies in life.

This, then, is the condition of things: men are launched into this world in large, in ever increasing numbers; men have necessities—the two most essential of which are space to hold, and food to sustain, their bodies. The Lord of the Manor, and his class, being possessed of the surface of the earth, are therefore possessed of that which, alone, can satisfy these requirements; they hold in their hands the granting of that without which life would be impossible;

and they grant this to the multitudes only on
condition of the payment of tribute—tribute
sufficient to enable them to satisfy, without labor on their part, not only their necessities, but
any desire, any whim, their fancy may suggest.

*   *   *   *   *

The Lord of the Manor is not the sole bene-
ficiary in this admirable scheme of tribute-levy-
ing.   He has associates who share, in a more or
less degree, and with slight variations, the same
conditions of life which he enjoys.

While a certain portion, however small, of
this earth is essential as a domicile for each in-
habitant thereof; while a certain amount of food
is necessary to sustain him, there are other things
which, in the civilized state, are required by
man.   These are the products of nature in a
form other than the raw material.   Some are
converted into raiment to cover the human
body; others into a more wholesome and agreeable substance for consumption.   The conver-
sion of these into their new forms, and their
distribution to the masses who required them,
was not to be a philanthropic operation.   To
trace the history of this operation is to trace
the origin and the development of the manu-
facturer and the merchant, who play such an

important part in our day. The first took
charge of those products which either had to be
prepared before being consumed, or had to be
manufactured before they could be worn; the
second undertook the distribution of all these.
Both had in view the disposing of same at a
profit.

As population increased and, in consequence,
as the demand for the means of subsistence
augmented; as science progressed and made
new discoveries in the methods of extracting
the produce and of converting it into the forms
necessary for consumption or for wear; as new
and more rapid means of transportation and
distribution were put in operation, the manu-
facturer and the merchant were enabled to
handle and control ever increasing quantities of
material. The more they handled and controlled, the greater the profits they realized.
These profits accumulating, soon gave them
wealth beyond their necessities. The ownership of this accumulated wealth was one of the
causes which brought into existence the class
known as capitalists—money-kings—who, having acquired, by means of profit in dealing in
the produce of the soil, riches as considerable as
those acquired by means of rent, by the owners

of the soil, were destined to become powerful rivals of the latter.

The money-king, with his capital, found himself in the same position as the Lord of the Manor with his land; he had more than he required for his personal use. But this, far from being an incumbrance, relieved him, on the contrary, of an infinity of anxieties; above all, it relieved him of the necessity to labor.

Men must have money; for under the complex system which the needs of society gradually developed, money became essential in the transactions of life, in the production, and more especially in the exchange, of the necessaries of life; and there is, in consequence, a constant demand, an endless striving, for it. Not only this, but no property can be acquired, no edifice erected, no enterprise inaugurated, without its assistance. Men, therefore, requiring money, to whom should they naturally go, to satisfy this need, but to him who has more than he himself requires?

The money-king thus becomes a personage of note, wielding immense power. He takes his place by the side of the Lord of the Manor; and as though it were the result of association, he adopts the methods employed by the latter.

Having taken due precaution for its protection and return, he lends the capital of which he has surfeit and which he, personally, cannot employ. As for the use of land, tribute is paid to the one, in the form of rent; so for the use of gold, tribute is paid to the other, in the form of interest.

Interest has to be paid, as has rent—and its payment is no less inexorable; to be paid, it must be earned; to be earned implies labor. Thus labor becomes instrumental in making capital, as well as land, productive, and in furnishing revenues to their respective owners.

    *   *   *   *   *

The field continuing to prove an attractive and lucrative one, there still remained merchants, manufacturers, and others who, each in his sphere, continued their occupations—not, however, without casting an envious eye on their fortunate brothers who had been crowned money-kings. This eye was not solely envious, it was discerning. They admired the methods of the great landowner, of the successful capitalist, and took note of the results. Not only they admired these methods but—imitation being the highest form of flattery—they were tempted to imitate them. Since the multitudes seemed disposed to toil to support the few in leisure, why should not the merchant prince, and for that matter all industrial princes, join the royal circle, and wear crowns of their own? Moreover, their undertakings had become so stupendous, and their management so onerous, that while clinging to the profits, they became more and more anxious to be relieved of the anxiety and labors which the superintendence of their affairs and the amassing of their wealth entailed. Furthermore, was not expansion, the exploitation of vaster fields, the crushing out of petty rivals—who, like flies tormenting lions, were a source of discomfort and annoy- ance—a consummation to be desired; one likely to result in greater profits? More capital might be required—but were not the allurements offered overwhelming? The joint-stock com- pany—an impersonal, a soulless corporation— was conceived; it took its place among the realities of the world; it was destined to de- velop, to find favor, to become a powerful fac- tor in the affairs of men. By its operation, the merchant-prince, as well as all others who, by whatsoever means, have accumulated riches, are accorded the most coveted of privileges. Leaving responsibility and the supervision of operations to managers and subordinates, they gather in profits as the Lord of the Manor gathers in rents, as the money-king gathers in interest—all of which helps increase the stock of wealth, for the comfort and glory of the elect of Fortune.

Thus the example first set by the Lord of the Manor—the example which awakened the envy and stimulated the ambition of many—came to be successfully followed by the money-king and the merchant prince, and other children of Mammon who constitute that galaxy of fortunate mortals who live without work when all others must work to live; who enjoy the fruits of labor without the fatigues of labor; to whom the ownership, the sovereignty of this world is accorded as though it were their natural, their legitimate due. Thus the surface of this earth is possessed by one class; its produce is controlled by another; and although these two combined constitute but a small proportion of the race, all the forces of humanity are put into operation to render this planet—called man's— a fair, an attractive abode, wherein they may spend their days in pleasure and leisure.

CHAPTER III.

AN INQUIRY INTO THE CAUSE OF THE EXISTING STATE OF THINGS.

NATURE has allotted this earth, with all its luxuriance, its richness, its verdure, its variety and charm of scenery, to man, as an abode ; but she has imposed, as a condition of his tenancy, the payment of a tribute—call it rent, if you will—failing which, death is the penalty.   This tribute is Labor.

There is nothing more evident than that to maintain itself on this globe, mankind must work.   It is an edict of the Universal Power from which the race, as a whole, cannot escape. Nor is the opportunity furnished to forget the inexorableness of this edict.   Multitudes toil to extract nourishment from the earth to feed humanity, and nourishment being consumed as it is extracted, multitudes continue to toil to extract more, and this again is consumed.   As it is with food, so is it with raiment.   Millions of hands work to clothe the race, but raiment, like food, though in a minor degree, must be renewed. So, likewise, must the race be sheltered —and though man build his home of rock, time will compel him to repair the damages which the hand of Nature has inflicted. Air, fire, water, and the needs of existence constitute eternal elements of destruction and consumption, which demand eternal labor to restore and to reproduce what is being destroyed and consumed. Were the army of workers to cease their efforts for a single year, countless numbers would suffer; were they to desist for a decade, the race would perish or be reduced to the savage state.

Without labor, humanity would be breadless; without labor, humanity would be clotheless; without labor, humanity would be roofless. Unless cultivated, the richest soil remains unproductive; unless manipulated, the finest materials remain unwoven; unless disturbed by mighty forces, the quarries of the mountains, from which our palatial structures are built, would slumber in their recesses. Nineveh and its splendors, Babylon and its suspended gardens, Athens and its temples, Rome and its memory-inspiring monuments, Byzance and its domes and minarets—all the proud cities of this world were raised from the earth by the hand of Labor. The tapestries which adorn ancestral halls, the canvases on which the painter's art breathes life, the marble to which the sculptor's chisel has given human form, are the children of Labor. The strides of civilization, the light of science, the course of progress; wealth, art, and all the marvellous machinery which throbs and pants like living beings, can be traced to Labor.

The world is, and must remain, a vast workshop. All nature toils; the universe is emblematic of action; action is emblematic of life, of power; and yet there are men who deem toil debasing; who boast of never having toiled! There are men who, by some strange dispensation, are exempt from work; and, stranger still, the multitudes, who feed, who clothe, who provide shelter for mankind, allow those who are indolent to enjoy the richest results of labor; they allow them to sit at the banquet of life and partake of its plenteousness, while they, sons of toil, are awarded the crumbs.

On what grounds, it may be asked, does the human race, which holds its lease of this earth direct from Nature, and pays to her the tribute —the rent—she demands, pay, in addition to this, tribute to certain individuals of the race, without due consideration, without good and valid cause? Are these certain individuals the rightful owners of this earth; are they the anointed masters of men; are they the superiors of their fellows—the lights of mind, the giants of body? Do they hold from Nature the exclusive power to share in her rights and partake of her tribute? If not, how come they to be possessed of this fair earth; how come they to control the produce of the earth; how come they to be exempt from labor and yet to enjoy the best this earth affords; how, above all, come they to hold the vast multitudes who inhabit this earth, in subjection to their will and pleasure?

This they do; and for this there must be some great, some prevailing, cause.

*   *   *   *   *

If the mass of men, representing the larger and more powerful interest, took possession of this planet, controlled its destinies, claimed the best and the fairest as their share, and held the few in subjection to their will and pleasure, there would be no problem to solve; the cause of such a condition of things would be apparent to all. But there is a problem to solve, a cause to detect, when the reverse of this prevails— as does prevail on our globe.

Casting our eyes over the face of the earth, and contemplating productive labor associated with poverty, and non-productive idleness associated with wealth, we are led to inquire how this state of things, so detrimental to the welfare of the larger and more powerful portion of the race, originated in the past and was perpetuated, through the centuries, to the present day. We would know why it is the many have submitted to the few, the strong to the weak; why those who cultivated the soil and drew therefrom all its variety of nourishment, fed on crusts, while the indolent had surfeit of its choicest fruit; why those who weaved the finest cloths were draped in rags, while rich purple hung on idle shoulders; why those who, with the rough material of the quarries, built majestic palaces, lived in huts, while those who could not hew a stone, dwelt in palaces.

One class, not producing wealth, could not, on the general ground of equity, claim the wealth which another class produced. Hence, from this standpoint, it does not appear that the leisure element had right on their side. Nor had they might. The laboring element was, by far, superior in numbers and in strength.

There was, so far as the eye could discern, no edict of nature, no law of man, to enforce this state of things. Yet the many, apparently having right on their side, and certainly having might, submitted to it as though they deemed all the powers of heaven and earth combined to insist on its enforcement. Surely for this there must have been a cause—a great, prevailing, cause. Nor is it a weighty task, requiring elaborate search, to discern this cause. Those who have the appearance of right to animate them; those who have power to sustain them, and yet fail to use their power to enforce their right, must be slaves to Ignorance.

As man's superior intelligence places him above, and gives him dominion over all other living things; as it allows him to harness the physically more powerful ox and horse to his purpose; and, more than this, as it enables him to discover and control the blind forces of nature, and use them for his benefit; so, likewise, when various bodies of men crystallized into the social state, those who had superior intelligence rose above, and held sway over, the ignorant; they harnessed them, as they harnessed the ox and the horse, for their purpose, and used them, as they used all else, for their benefit.

Herein can we detect and trace the origin of

the subserviency of the many, in whom the intellectual development was small, to the few, in whom the intellectual development was relatively large.   It is owing to this that some rose higher than others, mastered and controlled them, and used them for their own advantage ; it was due to their ignorance that the multitudes cultivated the earth and allowed the choicest fruit to those who cultivated it not ; that they weaved the finest cloths and yet were draped in rags ; built palaces, and yet dwelt in huts.

*   *   *   *   *

To wander back, through the labyrinth of centuries, into the darkness of the Past, for the purpose of measuring the density of that darkness, were indeed an undertaking in which to lose one's self would be inevitable, were it not that we are enabled to borrow from the Present certain signs which may serve as guide-posts; also light, which will render our path less difficult.

If printing, that simplest, yet grandest, of inventions, was instrumental in facilitating the spread of thought, in awakening discussion, in stimulating learning, in diffusing knowledge; if steam, with its marvellous propelling power, has rendered travelling more easy and rapid and, in consequence, brought the mental advantages which observation and personal contact with various races and their customs afford, within the reach of greater numbers; if electricity, with its instantaneous flash, communicates to the entire world the course of events in every portion thereof; if it makes known the theories of philosophers, the discoveries of scientists, the speeches of statesmen, the doings of governments, and places before each man, in every corner of the globe, a succinct universal history of the previous day; if, under such favorable circumstances as these, ignorance is still to be met with; if, in the enlightened times in which we live, ignorance is, in some quarters, still dense; what, we may ask, must it not have been ere the beneficial uses of printing, steam, and electricity were revealed to man? What must it not have been when the population of this globe was subdivided into small groups of men—without a single book among them; perhaps not a single wise man among them— interested only in the daily humdrum of their own monotonous life; unaware of the doings, yes, of the very existence of the vast world around and beyond them; little to discuss, less to speculate on, nothing tangible to hope for;

lying prostrate before idols their own hands had wrought; reverencing, in solemn manner, the beasts of the earth, then worshipping with ardent soul the fire of heaven? Unclean, untutored, unspeakably ignorant—ignorant of all which we, to-day, have knowledge of; living in ages—dark ages—wherein it is difficult to imagine even the reflected light of the sun as shining on the gloomy abode of man—these primitive mortals, these argonauts of Humanity, turning their longing eyes to the firmament above, may have dreamt of immortality; but, while mortal, they were like the brutes who contested with them the mastership of this earth—unconscious of the true nature of their surroundings; satisfying their material appetites as best they could, while their intellects were undeveloped, inert, enshrouded—but, fortunately, not dead.

*   *   *   *   *

Let us invoke Fancy—which, though never ranked among the many gods to whom the human knee has bent, has the power of creating, destroying, or altering all things at will—and picture to ourselves this fair earth of man, embellished as we see it to-day, with its verdant fields, its luxuriant gardens, its hamlets, villages and cities, its noble structures and majestic palaces, revolving through space—a silent, deserted planet. No, neither silent nor deserted. The song of the bird in the forest, the roar of the lion in the desert, the soft music of the rippling streams, the mournful sounds of the rolling waves, are still heard as of yore; but the voice of man is hushed, his race is extinct. With man has vanished his laws and his traditions.

Having destroyed the old, let Fancy picture the creation of a new race, similar to the one that is gone, save that all its members are equally enlightened, and free from the thraldom of custom which, tyrant-like, imposes itself as a second nature on all who come within its reach.

Were it not useless to ask, unless indeed offence to reason were intended, whether, in disposing of that which they found on this earth, and which seemed to correspond with their wants, these newly-arrived mortals would allot that which is most desired by all to a privileged few, for all time, while the multitudes would not only be given that which is least desirable, but would be compelled to toil, so that their favored companions might be maintained in a state of repose and luxury? If, instead of universal peace and happiness, the end aimed at

3

were general turmoil and discontent, and all the
evils which these engender, such a course would
be wisely pursued and the contemplated result
unavoidably attained.   Not the forbidden apple
of Eden, but the golden apple of Discord would
introduce sin and calamity to the unfortunate
race, while Iniquity, usurping the throne of
Justice, would drive Harmony far from the
haunts of men.

Who, among these new lords of creation,
would be so bold as to suggest so perilous a
course, with no custom to serve as guide, no precedent to point to as authority?   What man,
no matter what his greed, his arrogance, would
venture to seize upon more than he could use,
while his companions had less than they needed?

On what grounds, these would ask, do you
propose disposing of things as though we were
of a different race, and as such should submit
to different conditions?   Why should you, who
have but one body to feed, one body to clothe,
one body to shelter, claim numerous loaves, numerous garments, numerous houses, while we,
with many bodies, are exposed to hunger, to the
chill of the night and the rigors of the storm?   If
we were destined to eat less than you, surely
our capacity for food would be less; if it were

ordained that we required less shelter and fewer garments than you, there would be distinguishing signs to indicate this fact. If the discerning power which gave four legs to the horse, that he might travel long distances, and mighty wings to the eagle, that he might reach high altitudes, had intended that we should toil, while you indulged in leisure, would it not have given us more feet, more hands, more strength, than to you? Nature has not overlooked the requirements of animals; nor has she been blind to those of men. Why, then, should the greed of the few be allowed to interfere with her provisions for all? Why should you claim the lion's share, while we are condemned, like curs, to wander in search of bones? If reason and equity are to be ignored, and physical strength is to be the test, why should not we, the more powerful of mankind, secure the coveted prey, as do the more powerful beasts?

But Fancy, however subtle its tricks, however potent its sway in the realms of Fiction, must, perforce, retreat when confronted by Reality.

The race which first inhabited this earth, though superior in intelligence to all else living thereon, was an infant, and consequently an untutored, race. Hence there was no equitable

allotment of what was found on this earth.
There was no division having for object the en-
couragement, the development, of energy, industry, and genius.   There was not, for obvious
reasons, any system, based on social experience,
tending toward the general welfare.   There
were no guiding stars, no benevolent spirits, to
indicate the course men should pursue; to
direct them in their intercourse with each other;
to assist them in laying the foundations of a
social structure, which should offer shelter and
protection to all.

The earth had sprung from the womb of chaos,
and there was yet much of chaos clinging to
the earth.   Order and harmony were yet to come
forth to perform their duties toward the new-
born race, and assist in its nursing, education,
and final development.   Things were left to
shift for themselves; and men roamed about,
as did the beasts of the fields, attracted here
and there by such products as nature offered
freely to satisfy their necessities, and maintain
their existence.

But, as the child is gradually weaned from
his mother's breast, and must, in the course of
time, depend on his own efforts to secure nutrition, so the human race was gradually weaned

from the nourishment which mother earth offered spontaneously. The land had to be cultivated, and the food to sustain man drawn therefrom by man's own exertions. The shelter which the forest trees afforded was doomed to prove insufficient, and the skins of animals, which covered the body, to be cast aside for less primitive garments. New energies were called into play; also new faculties; all tending to the arousing, the development of intelligence. Those whose minds were most active, most receptive, most inventive; those who had the gift of initiative, were destined, at that early period, to lead the others, and eventually to master them. What wonder, then, that, proving themselves more capable than their fellow-men, they should have claimed advantages over them? What wonder, as centuries elapsed, and order and harmony began to conquer the lingering elements of chaos, and force mankind to adopt the social state, that those among them who could step forth with the mark of superiority on their brows, the evidence of superiority in their thoughts and in their deeds, the facility of expression, and the power of argument, on their lips, should have been accorded leadership; should have claimed more loaves, more garments, more houses, than those whose inferiority of mind required that they should be guided and commanded—that they should follow and obey? Nor does it appear that the latter, in accepting these conditions, considered that a wrong was being done them. Oppression will drive even the weak to resist the strong. It is, therefore, not probable that a conscious injustice would have been long tolerated by a large body of men capable of crushing those who inflicted it. Moreover, the advantages of wealth and of power were ever before their eyes, and unless so blinded as not to see them, the incentive to acquire these advantages was not missing. Hence, they had power; they had incentive ; yet they failed to use their power, and the incentive failed to move them.

Is it not safe to conclude, under these circum-stances, that the early submission of the majority, *as a body*, to the minority, is irrefutable evi-dence of mental inferiority on the part of the former ; that if there was not an equal division of the wealth of the world, it was because there was a natural inequality between men, which justified the unequal division ; that while— owing to the subsequent introduction of arbi-trary laws tending to maintain the *status quo*, and exclude new-comers—intelligence did not always succeed in rising to the surface, igno-rance, with rare exceptions, was a heavy weight which kept its unfortunate victims in the lower levels of life?

CHAPTER IV.

THE DIFFUSION OF KNOWLEDGE AND THE REVOLUTION IT IS PRODUCING.

A S we contemplate the history of the Past, the almost interminable vista of darkness, during which the mass of men seemed to slumber, is not the only one which arrests our attention. There flashed, now and anon, across the sombre firmament of Ignorance, a genius who, like a meteor shooting through space, left a trace of radiance in his wake. There arose, from among the multitudes, students and philosophers, scientists and dreamers, striving for knowledge, panting for truth. But their soaring minds dwelt mainly among the stars, or contemplated the mysteries of Fate and the blind forces of nature far more seriously and assiduously than they did the physical powers, and the legitimate aspirations, of man. They advanced theories, claimed principles, built systems, which they deemed eternal, and which subsequent generations saw levelled to the ground and scattered to the winds. Once in a while, fragments of the whole remained, and helped increase the small store of positive knowledge; but how infinitesimal was this when compared with the mass of fiction, of falsehood, of superstition—piled heaven-high— the accumulations of ages of ignorance!

The students, the philosophers, the scientists, the dreamers, were few, while those whose minds were inert were numerous. Scarcely did these hear the sounds which emanated from the elevated regions of Intellect; and those who did, grasped not their meaning; and, slaves to custom, they kept plodding on their weary way, as they had plodded for centuries past.

Thus while a small band—stimulated by a hidden power, which seemed to urge them on; and often receiving, as sole reward for their labors, the smile of the great and the patroniz- ing favors of those who shared in the division of the good and the fair things of life—were striving to make advances in the intellectual world, the mental, as well as the material, con- dition of the masses remained unaltered. Pro- gress, however small, however slow, was made, or attempted, in every science, save in that one which concerned the general welfare of the race.

True, an occasional voice was heard, a daring hand was raised, in the endeavor to arouse the multitudes from their lethargy and to improve their condition ; but the impulse had not fully matured ; development was incomplete, and the efforts, crushed in their infancy, were unproductive of results.

Similar, however, to Nature's mighty, though silent, operations, marvellous things were being prepared by unseen, unheard, human forces. The time came when phenomena, unprecedented and full of meaning, began to manifest themselves. The stagnancy of centuries was disturbed ; mental activity became prevalent; expectancy beat in every pulse ; hope swelled in every breast. All eyes wandered to the horizon, as though in search of something that must soon appear, and lo ! a rising orb was seen to drive the shades of night from the long-darkened firmament; an unknown light spread over the face of the earth, penetrated the souls of men, and gave new color to all things. A cycle was completed, and evolution made a step forward in its mysterious course. A new day was born for Humanity. An epoch was at hand wherein memorable events were to be recorded in the annals of Time; for the sun of Knowledge had risen, and the reign of Ignorance was measured.

*   *   *   *   *

In the last century, the world witnessed the commencement of the period—distinguished above all others—when the formerly limited sphere of learning, of investigation and enlighten- ment, was to be enlarged; when the barriers which excluded the mass of men from that sphere, were to be removed; when the inestima- ble value of Printing was to be finally realized; when its long deferred triumph was to be celebrated; when its empire, and the momentous changes which it implied, were really to begin.

Not only were great truths discovered, but great falsehoods, inherited from the earliest ages, were unmasked and eventually cast aside with the idols of antiquity; Philosophy took new wings and soared to strange and heretofore unexplored realms; Science expanded its do- minion and sought fresh fields of discovery; it advanced, step by step, until it burst, in the increased fulness of its development, into the glorious rays which illumine our present day, and brought into deeper contrast the dimness of the past. The age of Fiction and Sentiment seemed to be vanishing; that of Reality and Utility to be approaching. The conditions of society, the relations of its members and of its institutions to each other and to the state, the prerogatives of kings, the rights of men, and other kindred subjects came to the surface, and occupied the minds of all. The thoughts of the wise and of the benevolent were sent forth to the multitudes, and found an echo in the remotest hamlets. The dissemination of ideas provoked discussion; discussion stimulated inquiry; inquiry sharpened intelligence, and intelligence, directed in a new course, began to open the eyes of the people to the fact that the unfavorable conditions to which many of them had long submitted, were not the result of divine dispensations—eternal and immutable—but of human regulations, ephemeral and changeable.

And what are we called upon to relate as the foremost result of the diffusion of Knowledge? A solemn, an awe-inspiring protest against the ancient state of things. Murmurs arose which, feeble at first, grew louder and more frequent. From many quarters, sounds, like those of the clarion, were heard, and, wherever heard, men were stirred to action. The land became like a vast camp aroused from a heavy sleep. The elements of discontent gathered ominously; they increased with appalling rapidity, and finally broke out into a surging storm between the conflicting sections of society. The world witnessed a revolution, more universal, more pregnant with eventual results to the race, than any convulsion of nature.

The problem before us is, therefore, a clear one; the solution of which is correspondingly clear.

In examining the constitution of the social body, we have seen the strange spectacle of the more numerous and powerful portion of society submitting to conditions detrimental to themselves and beneficial to the smaller and weaker portion; we have become convinced from the brief and cursory survey given (and a more profound and elaborate survey could but result in deepening the conviction) that this state of things could never have obtained, had not the majority been less knowing, less intelligent, than the minority.

Ignorance, then, was the cause; the abject state was the effect. Since ignorance is vanishing, must not the conditions which sprung from ignorance also vanish? The cause disappearing, can the effect remain? Will not the awakening of the human race which led to the scientific, industrial, social, and political revolutions, lead to that one which, from a material standpoint, will prove most beneficial to the people—an economic revolution? In fact, is not the latter the logical, the inevitable, sequence of the former?

The answer to this is to be found in the tendencies of the times; it is revealed in the pages of history, which show that ever since means were adopted to diffuse knowledge, a movement, sometimes demonstrative, explosive, destructive, more often subdued and silent, but none the less objective, has been developing against the order of things whereby—owing to certain laws, customs, and traditions, and not to natural superiority—the desired things of this world are concentrated in the hands of the few and excluded from the many.

If the horse, more powerful than man, were to become as intelligent, would he consent to be harnessed under the same conditions as formerly? Would he submit to unfair treatment from one mentally his equal, physically his inferior? It would be unwise to expect this of the horse; it would be folly to demand it of man.

CHAPTER V.

PREMONITORY SIGNS.

WHEN earth-pervading, heaven-aspiring Knowledge, weary of its solitude and seclusion, escaped beyond the gloomy walls of cloister and the dingy garrets of student and philosopher; when, realizing its freedom, it wandered into peaceful village and crowded city, and became a thing of note, of observation and discussion; when, in its progressive course, it met the opposition of its arch-enemy, Ignorance, and following an irresistible impulse, cast down, with haughty defiance, the gage of battle; then, on this planet named Earth, was inaugurated a warfare in which no flag of truce was to be raised, no armistice discussed, no treaty of peace signed—a duel to the death between Knowledge and Ignorance.

The intellectual revolution against the reign of Ignorance is, by nature, destructive as well as constructive in its tendencies. It has been going on for many years, imperceptible to the

ordinary eye, subverting or altering all previous
notions and creeds, systems and institutions;
expanding the horizon of the human mind, and,
in respect to social and economic matters, point-
ing unmistakably to the gradual disappearance
of those conditions which sprung into existence
in unenlightened periods of the past.

Do we not already contemplate, in many
lands, the ruins of the forms of the old order?
Have we not seen the adoption of forms fore-
casting a new system, not yet in existence, but
which the logic of events is destined to bring
into existence—shadows, as it were, of events
to come?

In the historic hall where, in the midst of
national perturbation and expectation, the
French States-General met, a century ago, the
Commons insisting on the same privilege as
that enjoyed by the First and Second Estates,
of remaining covered in the presence of the
King, was a petty thing in itself; but how
pregnant with meaning, how fruitful of incidents!

From that date on, many changes were
wrought which indicate the advent of an era
strikingly different, in many respects, from the

one that is vanishing. These changes bear, all of them, the imprint of a dominant purpose, and betray the underlying tendency of the movement of the times—namely, the restriction of the undue advantages enjoyed by the few, and the increase of opportunities for the many to rise; in other words, the lessening of the great contrasts in the conditions of men.

If this was not the case, why should the towering influence of the Crown have been torn down, and the sovereignty of the people proclaimed? Why should titles of nobility, which implied differences in the social world, have been abrogated, and the name of citizen applied to all? Why should certain laws and usages, which gave privileges to some and denied them to others, have been abolished? Why should the great and the wealthy have eventually abandoned, in public, the gaudy dress and adornments which were the insignia of superior position in life? Lastly, why should the people, unless they resented, and wished to destroy offensive contrasts, have adopted, as the national device, the all-significant words, which adorn the edifices of man as well as the temples of God—

Liberty, Equality, Fraternity?

4

And following events down to our day, do we not realize, as enlightenment increases, an increasing tendency to free the mass of the population from the disadvantageous situation they formerly occupied ?   Have not the so-called middle classes risen to the point to which they long aspired ?   Have they not achieved a substantial, a magnificent, victory, while the world has resounded—till the sound has grown wearisome from its monotony—with what is fondly termed the triumph of Democracy ?   Is not the body of voters growing gradually larger and larger, thus increasing the number of those who are admitted factors in government ?   Was not a long and bloody war, involving thousands of lives and millions in money, considered opportune and justifiable in the emancipation of slaves ?   Is not serfdom abolished ?   Have not the foremost nations of civilization come face to face with something more than the mere spectre of socialism, which, aiming to relieve mankind of all the ills and iniquities which have oppressed them in the past, proposes the complete subversion of the existing order of things ?

Actual changes there have been, in truth, in one direction at least, and glaring presages of changes in many directions ; while it is obvious to all that things have progressed to the point where the all-absorbing question of the times is no longer the divine rights of kings, but the human rights of the peoples of the earth.

CHAPTER VI.

MODERN DEMOCRACY THE RESULT OF THE DIFFUSION OF KNOWLEDGE.

HOWEVER clear the cause of the political and other disturbances which agitated Europe and America a century ago,—and which constitute the most remarkable period of all history—their effect cannot fail to perplex us if we look at them as independent movements. If, however, we consider them, as they should be considered, as initial steps in a vast forward movement, as mere incidents of a general revolution, still in progress, still to fulfil its purpose, perplexity gives way to easy comprehension.

Men, at that time, though unprepared to solve the crisis which came upon them, were nevertheless resolved to meet it with the courage and the lights they then possessed. Human affairs had reached a stage when innovation was found to be necessary. The spirit of change was abroad; also the powers to effectuate a change.

Event followed event in rapid succession ; so likewise suggestions of what changes to make ; and formulas innumerable from innumerable quarters.

The agitation spread, in a more or less marked degree, over the civilized portions of the world. It resulted, generally, in a realization of the power of the people and, consequently, in a fuller recognition of their rights. It proved conclusively that there was, on the face of this earth, a set of men, other than princes and privileged orders, who were entitled to recognition and, if need be, could demand, and enforce, recognition.

One result was hailed by the multitudes with emotions of joy and hope, and was watched by the ruling classes with alarm and distrust. The former thought it would, more than aught else, promote their elevation ; the latter apprehended that its success implied their downfall. This result was the adoption, after many reactionary attempts, of the popular, in lieu of the former, system of government.

Obviously, the objections on the dominant side were based less on the mere change of form, than on the fear lest the newly accredited sovereign people—the makers of governments, of laws, or the unmakers thereof—with their recently acquired knowledge, their numbers, their right and their might, should not remain content with the semblance of sovereignty, while certain favored citizens enjoyed the substance, the real power, and all the advantages these bring.

Two powerful republics were established : one in a country whose people had, for genera· tions, been familiar with monarchical institu· tions ; the other in a Land of Promise which, since the native Redskin had laid down the sceptre, had been considered the fairest colony of the vastest empire of the earth.

These two republics were, unlike the more ancient ones of Italy, democratic in form. It was freely declared that the machinery of State was not to be used, as formerly, for the benefit of a few, but for the benefit of all the governed —thus acknowledging the supremacy of the nation. Herein we detect premonitory symp· toms of an attempt to eliminate one of the effects which had sprung from the ignorance of the people, and to confer on them some of the advantages which their new acquirements en· titled them to.

The advent of Democracy, not by the sudden

coup of an ambitious leader, anxious to win popular favor; not as a political experiment; but as the inevitable consequence of a new condition of things which is daily becoming more and more palpable, is, in itself, evidence of the intellectual progress of the people, and indicates beyond doubt that their enlightenment must result in their elevation, just as their ignorance had resulted in their abasement.

It was natural that, as knowledge spread, a revolt should have been inaugurated against the absolutism of monarchy, which implied popular subjection, and in favor of its substitute, which implied popular emancipation. Hence it was that, in the two countries referred to, the system of government adopted was democratic in form. Be it observed, however, that it was democratic in form only—not in substance. Had it, from its incipiency, been the latter as well as the former, then would have been accomplished, in a remarkably short period, the most remarkable revolution conceivable; then would social evolution have progressed at a rate totally incompatible with the magnitude and importance of the change to be wrought; then would Humanity, still in the infancy of its new life, have accomplished a task which time and experience alone could accomplish; then, contrary to all phenomena attending great movements, would a people who had long been ignorant, and submitted to the conditions which ignorance imposes, have sprung, in one bound, into a state of complete enlightenment, and enjoyed the conditions which enlightenment demands.

To have expected this, would have been to look for the cessation of those laws of nature which require the gradual development of all things—from the blade of grass to the mighty oak—and especially of those things which are destined to last, to brave the storms of the elements and the ravages of time.

As the seed of Democracy had to be planted ere it could grow, so is it necessary that its growth shall reach a certain point before it bear fruit.

CHAPTER VII.

THE TRIUMPH OF DEMOCRACY, SO FAR, A TRIUMPH OF MERE FORMS.

WHILE the ancient régime has been changed in various respects and, if we consider how slow, how gradual, as a rule, are all human innovations, changed with marvellous swiftness; while events, some foreseen, others unlooked for, have come to pass—undoing much that had been done; nullifying much more— flux and reflux in the great movement forward, in the widespread revolution which the stimulus to learning has inaugurated in the affairs of men; yet if we, at the end of this nineteenth century, cast a glance of scrutiny over those lands where the triumph of Democracy and the sovereignty of the people are most loudly proclaimed, we find, wherever we gaze, a state of things strikingly similar, in its essential respects, to that which existed prior to these changes. No haughty monarch, no frivolous court, it is true; but now, as then, we see vast riches in the hands of the few, and dire poverty facing the many; we see, now as then, an enormous distance dividing the two extremes in the social sphere—zenith and nadir—one so high as to dazzle the sight of those below; the other so low as to be scarcely noticed by those above. We realize, in one word, that while the spread of knowledge and the consequent awakening of intelligence, created a tendency to bring about an equitable levelling of conditions, this tendency has, so far, touched mainly the surface of things; we find that the forms of the old order have been annulled, while the substance remains; and that the forms of a new order have been adopted, while the substance is still absent.

There has been a levelling in titles, there has been a levelling in dress, there has been a levelling, more apparent than real, in the application of the law; there has been a levelling, absolutely fictitious in its results, in the distribution of political power; but as regards the ownership of this earth and its riches (and reflect well, O Reader, how more important than all others is this last, on this planet of ours!) there has been little or no attempt at levelling. Contrasts in everything are less glaring, save in wealth—the great, the dominant power—which purchases everything this world produces, everything this world can give.

Thus, while the fair land which once knew proud princes and resplendent courts, now knows princes and courts no more, while the land which once witnessed the most brilliant array of nobles of which history relates, now looks on their descendants as they would on the ruins of a dead age; while the land which was once familiar with feudalism, with class distinctions and high privileges, rose from the smoke of battle and the blood and turmoil of revolution, bearing on its standard, which it aimed to make the standard of the world, "Liberty, Equality, Fraternity," there are still, in this fair land, geniuses who, being slaves to poverty, must doff the cap to fools who are masters of wealth; there are so-called plain citizens who would not surrender the title to their possessions for all the titles of nobility of ancient and modern times; there are distinctions of condition based in no sense upon merit, natural superiority, or public service. In that which is most essential to the material welfare of man; in that which decides whether his life shall be one of ease, of comfort, of luxury, or one of labor, of anxiety, and want, there has been no equitable levelling, no destroying of glaring contrasts.

In the face of these facts, there are those (whose vision is as restricted as that of the peasants who imagine the mountains of their valley to be the limits of the earth) who believe and proclaim that the events referred to are the limits of human possibilities; that the advent of Democracy implies the actual triumph of Democracy; that because political independence has been achieved, monarchy abolished, and republics established, the *summum bonum* of nations has been attained; that the surging wave of revolution which has swept over the land, has expended itself, and having landed man on the highest possible plane of human prosperity and contentment, he has every reason to be satisfied with things as they are; and, consequently, it were futile for him to hope or to strive further to improve his condition.

Strange illusion! and yet not strange when we consider that we live in a world swayed for ages by forms, and guided by words; a world incapable, at first sight, of distinguishing between the shadow and the reality of things, between the meaning of phrases and the fulfilment of their meaning.

*   *   *   *   *

If under monarchical absolutism the King's power was paramount to that of his subjects ; if the people's welfare was subordinate to that of the sovereign and of the privileged classes ; if the laws favored the latter and were mainly for their benefit and protection ; then the triumph of Democracy over monarchical absolutism implies that the people's power shall not be subordinate to that of any individual, nor their welfare to that of any class ; it implies, above all, that the spirit of the laws shall tend toward the greatest good of the greatest number.

The triumph of Democracy, if it be a substantial and not an imaginary one, means not only that there shall be no privileged nobility and clergy, as formerly, but that no set whatever of citizens shall enjoy inordinate, and especially unearned, advantages over their fellow-citizens ; it means deviation from that system of government which tolerated gross inequalities in the conditions of men, regardless of their merits ; it involves the securing to all of fair opportunities in the race for the prizes of life ; it implies the discontinuance of that state of things which allowed the accident of birth, the favoritism of princes, or the caprice

of Fortune, to become instrumental in raising
a few immeasurably above all others ; which not
only assured the few the enjoyment of great
wealth and great favor with government, but
permitted them, at their death, to transfer these
to heirs ; and which, by maintaining all privileges and advantages in the hands of a class,
aimed to make them perpetual, and thus per-
petually exclude the majority of men from participating therein.   If Democracy does not mean
the cessation of these conditions, it means nothing ; if it does not aim to accomplish this end,
it is a sham, an illusion, a misnomer.

This state of things having existed under
monarchical rule, it was, it is fair to assume, to
destroy it that monarchy was abolished in certain countries, and democratic rule substituted
in its stead.   It was because the French nation,
long restless under the yoke of tyranny, had
become more fully informed of the abuses and
iniquities of the system under which they lived,
that they rose in a body to overthrow it.   Indeed, so resolute were their efforts to eradicate
the ancient evils ; so heroic, in appearance, were
the remedies applied; so fierce was the struggle against their oppressors, that the world,
unaccustomed to the sight, stood aghast, and
looked on in amazement.

Proud in the display of their power, rejoicing in the victory they imagined they had achieved, the people returned to their workshops and their fields, and awaited the coming of the Golden Era.

The Golden Era never came ; and no wonder !

This mighty revolution, with its vast upheaval of passions and moral forces; its demolition of prisons and overthrowing of thrones; its denial of God and deification of Reason; its days of terror and scenes of horror; its wild shouts of exultation and weird hymns of triumph; this revolution, so far-reaching in its conceptions, so universal in its aspirations for the emancipation, for the welfare, of Humanity —what did it accomplish? Obviously not that which it set out to accomplish; certainly not that in which the welfare of Humanity was most seriously involved: a fairer division of man's earth and its wealth. True, Monarchy was erased and Democracy substituted in its place ; but a change of name could not effect a change of condition. Diogenes apostrophized as Crœsus would still remain poor, and Crœsus as Diogenes be none the less rich.

The people ceased to be the subjects of haughty kings ; they remained subject to haughty laws. They won a crown, but no dominion; acquired sovereignty, yet retained their poverty.

Aside from such natural advantages as the country may afford, do the masses of to-day, under democratic rule, differ strikingly from the masses under kingly rule? Do the favored few enjoy less wealth, less luxuries, less influence? The glories of monarchy have departed, but the miseries of the people remain; the contrasts which offended their sense of right and aroused their just resentment, are still visible on all sides; they are as overshadowed to-day by an opulent class as they were formerly by a noble class. Rapaciousness, in the upper circles, far from diminishing, has increased; greed is allowed to run unbridled by any law. The favorites of Industry have outstripped the favorites of Royalty. They, too, are permitted to feed on the public, and grow rich at their expense. They, too, dwell in palaces, are surrounded by magnificence, and display their affluence as though to mock those from whom they draw their revenue. They realize profits and amass fortunes which bring out, with renewed vividness, the difference between the two elements of society, the rich and the poor. Now, more than ever, is accumulation and waste seen on one side, want and suffering on the other. The artificial is dominant and Mammon is king. On him has fallen the mantle of sov-ereignty; before him the respectful bearing; to him the obsequious bow. Everything is brushed aside to make room for the Majesty of Wealth.

Wherein, then, so far as actual, tangible, ef-fects go, consists the much talked of superiority of the republican over the monarchical system? Is it that the civil list of a president is trivial compared with that of a prince; his functions less imposing, his surroundings less magnificent? Here, at least, is a lesson rich in meaning, if not in results. Here is a tacit admission that reck-less extravagance, in certain quarters especially, is an audacious contrast to, and a constant mockery of, the poverty of the people. But what, beyond a mere moral lesson, is taught by curtailing the expenditures of one individual, and making him, who should shine above all others, a solitary example of the sin of extrava-gance? He is denied a royal revenue and the splendors of a court; the nation over which he rules—with a power and responsibilities greater than those of many modern sovereigns—is termed a Republic; and it is claimed, in conse-

5

quence, that gigantic strides have been made in the art of government. In what respect? Titles, which in themselves are harmless, are abolished; the privileges of excessive wealth, which are a public danger, are maintained; shadows are attacked, substances are left untouched; Monarchy is overthrown as the oppressor, the Republic is acclaimed as the benefactor, of the people; yet this people-loving, this king-hating, Republic, shelters a host of proud money-kings who, conscious of power derived from state support, lord it over the land; it tolerates, in the face of struggling multitudes, a class of favored citizens who enjoy princely incomes and indulge princely excesses; it suffers them to form combinations whereby they are enabled to exercise the sovereign right of levying on the governed, and taxing them, in various ways, for their personal support and aggrandizement.

If this be the triumph of Democracy, in what direction shall we look for the apotheosis of Plutocracy?

The people, the sovereign people, are still ruled by laws inherited from the Past, when they had no voice in government; the latter's main purpose is the preservation of existing economic conditions, and the protection of prop-

erty as at present distributed—the greater
and better portion of which is in the hands
of a class, and is being there concentrated.
Wander through Republics, Monarchies, and
Empires, the world over; everywhere will the
same dominant purpose be found.

Who, then, dares assert that government is
for the benefit of the majority, when its first
concern is wealth, of which the majority have
little or none? What matters it, then, to these,
who presides over their destiny, a potentate in
royal robes, or a crownless chief, so long as
their destiny, under whatever rule, remains
unchanged?

A popular government is one based on the
popular will; it is an instrument whereby the
will of the people, in the form of laws, is enforced. Where, on the face of this broad earth,
is such a government to be found? Where the
one, however democratic in name, which is not
an instrument, as are monarchies, to protect the
interests, the privileges, of the few? Where
the land, the happy land, whose laws provide
the greatest good for the greatest number?

Yet the majority are said to rule.

Eccentric majority!

*　　*　　*　　*　　*

Society, in the so-called blessed lands where Democracy reigns, is, it is claimed, an association of men under a government having for object the welfare of all the members constituting said association. The welfare of all is the logical purpose of association ; it is the first object of government. If, then, the aim of a Democracy be the welfare of all, or of the majority of, the members of the society of which it is composed, is it not pertinent to ask whether it is consistent, under its rule, to allow a few of the members to accumulate, out of the general wealth, more riches than they can dispose of, while others, no less intelligent and far more industrious, have less than they need ? If its purpose be the suppression of a favored class, and the elimination of all distinctions and privileges, unmerited and unearned, is it not relevant to inquire whether it is consistent, under its rule, to tolerate the existence of a class who enjoy the distinction and privilege of being born to a life of leisure and luxury, when the majority of men, members of the same association, are born to a life of labor and discomfort ? If its object be the establishment of fair opportunities for all, is it not proper to ask whether fair opportunities exist where the advantages of inherited wealth are pitted against the disadvantages of inherited poverty; where the few are armed from head to foot for the contest of life, while the many have nothing to shield them but their native ardor and intrepidity? Is it consistent with the purposes, the principles, of Democracy—which has cast aside Aristocracy, and affects to hold it in contempt—to permit a few favorites of Fortune to live and act as though they were exalted by nature above their fellow-men, and to enjoy such a position of vantage that they are enabled to play an important, though often concealed, part in the management of public affairs, in the election of legislatures, in the control of government; and, under the ægis of modern Democracies, to wield a power greater, in some respects, than that of the privileged classes under the Aristocracies of old?

It is obvious that if the promoters of these Republics, which were to open before an astonished, if not admiring, world, a new and better era of government, had any special object in throwing off the old form of government and adopting the new, it was an object they deemed unattainable under monarchy, since they emphatically repudiated monarchical principles and

tendencies. This object, under popular government, could be no other than the advancement
of the general interests in opposition to the
personal interests of the King and of the privileged classes, which were paramount under former governments; any other object than this
could have been attained without change of
government and without flourish of trumpets.
But casting aside the high-sounding phraseology
of declarations and proclamations, which char-
acterized those days, and considering only the
plain facts, the results, as they stand before us,
what shall we say of the promoters of these republics? Were they, with all their courage,
lacking in the boldness required to strike off
those features of the old order which time and
custom had ingrafted on social institutions, but
which were, nevertheless, the most objectionable
features thereof?   Were they so closely linked to
the former régime, that the bandage had not
fallen from their eyes, and they were blinded to
the true state of things?   Or, alarmed at the
spirit of revolution and innovation which was
in the air, and fearing it might engender excesses
dangerous to the public weal, were they induced
to use their influence to confine it considerably
within its logical bounds, rather than allow it

to trespass beyond these? Is it not, on reflec-
tion, clear that the time, as stated elsewhere,
was not fully ripe for the complete change;
that they merely sowed a seed which the future
would see grow and bear fruit; laid foundations
on which others would be called upon to build,
and did for their generation what the conditions
of the period permitted? It is certainly difficult
to reconcile, at first sight, many of the inconsistencies which pervade their proclamations, and
render nil, or contradict, in some of their most
material points, several of the declarations they
enunciated concerning the rights of the people.
Thus, after declaring that *all men are born and
continue equal in rights*, they gravely affirmed
that property (which all men have not) is *an
inviolable and sacred right, of which no one can
be deprived.*

One man is born in penury, with all that penury implies; another is born in affluence, with
all the advantages affluence brings; one has before him a future of competition, of labor, of
striving to maintain existence; the other, by the
operation of the laws of inheritance, is destined
to partake, without labor, of all that is most desirable in life; one has rights which, being
shared by all men, none will envy; the other

enjoys privileges which, being denied the majority of men, the majority will covet; yet both
are said to be born and to continue equal in
rights!   The princely estates owned by the
heirs of mistresses of kings, are theirs by *sacred*
right ; the domains occupied by men whose ancestors received them as a reward for violating
the domains of political neighbors, are theirs by
inviolable right ; but what property, however
small, can many worthy sons of worthy sires
claim as their right ?

Social distinctions were declared to be purely
conventional, and as such were seriously condemned ; but what greater social distinction can
exist than that between the poor and the rich
man ; between the man who is compelled to
dwell in a hut, and the one who inherits a
palace ; between the man who, to live, must
work for others, and the one who is only content to live so long as he can get others to work
for him ?

The promoters of the Revolution, while claiming to aim at the abolition of all abuses, allowed
that one which towered above all others, and
which, more than all others, called for restric-
tive action, to stand unmolested, a threatening
danger to the rights, peace, and happiness of the
larger portion of the nation.

And are not our modern republics, with their proud boast of equality, their virtuous contempt of privilege, blind to the inequalities of wealth and the privileges of inheritance?

The right to own property is one which, as things now stand, the few inherit and the many must contend for; it is a right, similar in conditions, to a free-for-all race, but where all save the favorites are heavily handicapped; it is like a contest for prey between a hawk with swift wings and a hawk with clipped wings; it is a lottery in which nine out of ten of the rich prizes are allotted, in advance, to certain individuals, while for the tenth there are a million competitors. The blanks are numerous, and most of the minor prizes are so insignificant as to be unworthy the name.

Everything in sight, in the most desirable portions of the globe, is now held; what is not in sight is being diligently looked for by those who have the means to make searches, and the power to hold and develop whatever may be found. Where, then, are they who have no property to look for any? What, beyond bare subsistence, are they to compete for, to labor for? Of what avail is their energy, their intelligence, their genius? Though told that they are born equal in rights with other men, they cannot even hope to share equally with other men in the possession of this fair earth and the fruit it sends forth.

When one man is entitled to own a score of mansions, while many have no roof to shelter them ; to be lord of endless acres, while thousands have not a burial plot ; to indulge in waste, while multitudes are wanting ; is it not a privilege which partakes of the nature of flagrant abuse ? When it is further considered that this privilege is unlimited ; that it is unrestricted by any law ; that it is made perpetual by inheritance, can it be claimed that the government under which such a state of things exists, is popular in principle or democratic in practice ? When this excessive, and often unearned, privilege is enjoyed by a small minority of the governed and, under the conditions above referred to, is declared to be a right, "*sacred and inviolable*," is it not the sublimity of irony to allude to the rights of the majority ?

❖   ✳   ✳   ✳   ✳

If the will of the majority of the governed be the paramount law, surely that law, to be consistent, should conform with the interests of the majority ; the interests of the majority, if considered, call for the improvement of their condition; the improvement of their condition demands, as an initial step, legislation which shall curtail the privilege, now enjoyed by the minority, of absorbing such a vast quantity of that which is essential to ameliorate one's situation in life, that all others are deprived of the opportunity of acquiring a reasonable share thereof.

This legislation has not been forthcoming. Indeed it would appear, from the condition of things, that it was the few who controlled the making of laws, since the laws favor the few; and that the many had no voice in framing them, since they are the least benefited thereby. Thus are we brought face to face with the incongruous situation of the majority holding supreme power in the state, and consequently holding the means to dispose of things according to their interests, while the minority enjoy, in apparent security, all the advantages which supreme power can command.

Ever since the opening of the democratic era, the legislators of nations have been actively engaged revising old, and devising new laws. They assemble, with much solemnity, in imposing halls, and gravely discuss those matters which are supposed to concern the public weal. Generation

after generation of brilliant men—men of wealth
and high position—have contested the honor of
representing the people and legislating in their
behalf. Years upon years of study, research,
and debate have been required to accomplish
their task. Volumes upon volumes of reports,
amendments, repeals, and enactments stand as
evidence of their legislative labors. If, however,
we examine critically this stupendous work of
learned law-givers ; if we analyze it to probe its
nature, and reduce it to its simplest expression,
we find its component parts to be nothing more
than various kinds of dust, scientifically prepared for the people's eyes.

The mysterious councils of Zeus and his
Olympian group were wont to impress the
simple-minded Ancients with profound awe.
To the more enlightened Moderns they are,
however, a source of innocent merriment. And
so, no doubt, will future historians refer to the
meetings of those who now preside over our
destinies, and point, not without humor, to the
elaborate and protracted disputations, intended
to deceive expectant mortals into the belief
that momentous measures are being advocated
in their interest.

There have been endless discourses on various

subjects which may have increased the pride, but in no way augmented the income, of the masses of the population; there have been discussions on tariffs, on finances, on political matters, foreign relations, and on various taxes to be paid by the governed for the maintenance of government; but where, in the mass of legislation enacted, do we detect the much-needed economic reforms which, alone, can materially benefit the people at large? Where do we discern a serious attempt to establish something of a politic, something of an equitable, disposition of the property, of the goods, of the commonwealth?

All the legislation enacted since pseudo-popular parliaments have met, cannot compare, in point of vital importance, with the laws and usages still in force, whose origin antedates popular government. Yet the legislators meet regularly, at a great expense to the nation, and profess to legislate for the people. Far from promoting the interests of the latter, have they not attempted to mislead them by their impressive verbosity? Have they not, in imitation of the Barons of old, usurped the cloak of authority, and clothed themselves therewith? Have they not given closer attention to their personal welfare and advancement, than to those of their constituents from whom they hold power?

Well may it be asked, What have you, representatives of the people, done for the people? What action have you taken to curtail the privileges of the minority and promote the interests of the majority? What laws have you enacted whereby all men can discern, as they can day from night, the dividing line between the two great epochs of government by the will of the Absolute Monarch, and government by the will of the Sovereign People?

*   *   *   *   *

But does the responsibility for this inactivity rest with the legislators alone?

When the people acquired political power, they won a mighty weapon from their oppressors; but, like the South Sea Islander who playfully seized a pistol and deemed it a toy, they ignored its real uses; they have, so far, overlooked the sole purpose for which it was won—the advancement of their interests, the improvement of their condition. They are still held in subjection by the golden weapon, whose efficacy is so potent that, in the hands of the few, it awes the multitudes, and keeps them,

the so-called makers and destroyers of governments, at a distance—hat in hand, head bowed,
awaiting orders from their masters; they, the
rulers of to-day, have not yet changed, except
in name, the rule of yesterday, when they were
under the dominion of despots; the spirit of
the governments they overthrew still hovers
above, still dominates, them; wealth, the great
purchasing power, is as far from their reach
under the existing system as it was under the
tyrannical systems of the Past; the hated personal master is dead, but his impersonal succes-
sor, imperious Capital, still lives; they are his
servile subjects; they are harnessed to his gor-
geous chariot, victims of his pride and arrogance.

Of what avail is it, then, that they should
have revolted against despots, changed régimes,
and marched in triumph to legislative halls?
Have they not permitted those laws to stand
which allow the greatest privileges to the smallest number? Have they not, by their inaction,
left the greatest number where they have always
stood—in the vast arena of the world, face to
face with the wild beast, Hunger—while the
fat patricians, robed in purple, recline at their
ease, and look from afar at the battle of life?
Have they not, by failing to denounce and re-

ject them, given the stamp of approval to the fundamental principles of the form of government they repudiated? Have they not maintained the usages and traditions which empower the favored of Fortune to accumulate beyond their needs, and compel others, the unfortunates, to suffer from want?

If arbitrary rulers were overthrown by popular clamor, arbitrary laws are kept in force by popular silence, implying assent. These laws, whether written or unwritten, are the real oppressors, since they unduly favor the few; yet they, which alone can change the condition of the governed, remain unchanged. Being unrepealed, it is no less the duty of the republican executive to see them enforced, than it was formerly the duty of the royal executive. This being the case, is it not evident that the people's notable increase of power has not resulted in a corresponding increase of benefit? What have their votes, repeatedly cast, secured for them that they did not previously possess? Notwithstanding their commanding numbers, they are domineered over by a haughty caste; notwithstanding their supreme will, they are subjected to the will of others; they wander, in straggling bands, over highways they have traced, through vast and beautiful realms; they linger in cities they have built, within the shadow of palaces they have raised; they encounter on all sides wealth, luxury, and abundance; they hear sounds of revelry and, midst majestic splendors, witness regal entertainments; and they, the sovereign people, are begging for labor, grateful for bread to eat, for a roof under which to sleep—living proofs that

" Uneasy lies the head that wears a crown."

The hour has not yet sounded—and yet it is not distant—when they will awake to the knowledge that political rights were fought for, and won, to secure economic rights; when they will be convinced that their claims to sovereignty must remain chimerical so long as the supremacy of wealth is real, and its powers unrestricted; when they will demand that popular government cease to be a fiction, and become in fact, what it is in name, the people's, and not a class', government. Not until that hour has rung, shall Consistency and Reason cease revolting at seeing the flag of Democracy float over the land where Mammon is King.

6

CHAPTER VIII.

THE TENDENCIES OF THE TIMES POINT TO THE SUBSTANTIAL TRIUMPH OF DEMOCRACY.

SINCE, under our present Republics and popular governments, there still exists a class which enjoys the undue advantages and privileges which great wealth and unrestricted inheritance give; since the condition of the body of the people, no matter how industrious and educated they may be, still stands in bold contrast with that of opulent citizens; since the competition for the prizes of life is notoriously unequal and unfair and, consequently, all are not given the same opportunities to rise; since the democratic legislature is such only in name, as is shown by its failure to inaugurate legislation tending to better the situation of the nation at large; since political power in the hands of the people is, as yet, a mere form, as is evidenced by their failure to secure therewith the supremacy which is within their reach; it is manifestly premature to refer, at the present time, to the glorious triumph of Democracy and its wonderful achievements.

But are we to infer from the foregoing that, Democracy having proved a failure in the past, its cause is to be despaired of in the future; that because the people, though more enlightened, are still subjected to former unfavorable conditions, they will always so remain?

Astronomers assure us that if a distant star —colliding, may be, with some wandering comet —were to be scattered through the universe in infinitesimal fragments, its rays would still continue to vibrate through space and be visible to our eye many years thereafter. So, likewise, the evils which emanated from the depths of intellectual darkness must be expected to hover over the earth, and be felt for some time after that darkness has disappeared. But one thing is certain—and let its inevitableness be impressed on the minds of all men—as when the star became extinct, its light was destined to grow less and less, and finally to fade away for ever, so when Ignorance is stamped out, will its gloom be gradually dispelled, and the conditions which emanated therefrom vanish for all time.

The events which startled the world during

the last century, were but indications of the
dawn of a new day; they were the first spas-
modic movements of an awakening from a
protracted sleep; they were the first cry of
Humanity in the new life, the new career, that
then opened before it; they were the initial
steps towards the fresh fields which are being
opened and prepared for the nations of the
earth.

The man who, under the influence of a powerful opiate, has been slumbering for a long time,
does not, on first awakening, become fully conscious of his condition, or familiar with his surroundings; he looks around, with half-open
eyes, in a semi-bewildered state; the day, to
which he has so long been unaccustomed, dazes
him; if he attempts to rise, his head will reel,
his steps will be uncertain, he will stumble and
fall.   He does not grasp the succession, the order
of events, of things, or their true relation to each
other; he has not complete control of his
thoughts; hence his actions, his words, will appear inconsistent, eccentric.   Such was the condition of those nations which, under the influence
of that most powerful of opiates, Ignorance, had
been sleeping for centuries, when Knowledge,
acting as an antidote, aroused them from their

lethargy. Repeated convulsions of the social
organism gave evidence of a revival, an awakening; but the new light which had appeared
dazed them; their movements were erratic;
they rose and then fell, and rose and fell again.
They had not fully collected their thoughts, considered their situation, or planned their course.
The result was that while they acted, their
actions did not produce the anticipated effects.
The conditions which surrounded them were so
novel, the changes so sudden, the turmoil so
great, the opposition so concentrated, the senses
so excited, the passions so aroused, that judg-
ment lost its bearings, and the people became
bewildered. They were, as has been seen, more
impressed by forms than by substances, and directed their heaviest blows at the former. But if,
in their half-awakened condition, they thought it
was names, titles, outward forms, which brought
to their possessors the advantages of life, there
was some excuse for their so thinking; since in
many notorious instances the two were synonymous. Those whose fame had spread through-
out the land; those who basked in the sunshine
of the monarch's favor; those who lingered in
the delicious shades of the court of Versailles;
those whose mansions, whose estates, whose sur-

roundings, surpassed in grandeur and in extent
all others, were, in the public mind, intimately
associated with the resonance, the glamour, of
high-sounding names, titles, distinctions.   Hence,
in attempting to reduce the contrasts between
the various sections of society, in endeavoring to
establish greater *equality*, what wonder that the
people should have aimed their shafts at the
high places where titles and distinctions were
intrenched, and attacked those forms with which
they had always associated contrasts ?

Nor should it be overlooked that the class
who possessed wealth, without enjoying royal
favor, and who were held in contempt by the
privileged nobles, were not adverse to the abolishing of contrasts in forms—wherein they had
no share—so long as the contrasts in substances, in which they participated, remained.
This class played a significant rôle, not only in
subverting monarchy and the nobility, but in
misleading the multitudes.   They thought, only
too justly, that by attacking the forms which
the people had learned to look upon as the cause
of their abasement, they would be blinded to
the substances which were the real cause thereof.
In other words, they concluded that by cutting
short the reign of kings, they would be able to

inaugurate their own. How admirably they have succeeded in this needs no illustration.

Moreover, the gathering together, the consolidation, the drilling, of the multitudinous bodies which, before they could act wisely, consistently, had to act in concert, as though they had but one body, one mind, one will, one purpose, was a task not for a single, but for many generations to accomplish successfully. The innovations which the first victories of Knowledge over Ignorance were destined to achieve, could not, in the nature of things, be brought about instantly; the social fabric, with its complex and innumerable ramifications and connections, which it had taken centuries to construct, could not be altered in a day.

It were no less unreasonable to expect the triumph of Democracy at its birth, than to have expected Cæsar or Napoleon to perform, in their extreme youth, the marvellous deeds which crowned their manhood. They had within them—undeveloped, but yet growing—the qualities, the material, essential to the making of great conquerors, great rulers; but these qualities, this material, had to await the period of their full development; further still, they had to await the advent of opportunity.

But while others might have filled the place of the mighty conquerors and rulers, nothing on this earth can take the place of Democracy; for the latter means the supremacy, not of one man, not of one dynasty, but the supremacy of mankind, of the human race, in the control of the affairs of this world, in the disposal of its riches, in the awarding of its prizes. It has, what neither Cæsar nor Napoleon had, the right of succession ; it has legitimacy. Its advent to the throne depends not on fortuitous circumstances, but upon the inexorable logic of events. Although still in its youth, it already wears the crown and bears the title of sovereign. It awaits its majority to enter into full power, and control the revenues of its vast dominions. These revenues are still enjoyed by Plutocracy ; but is not this enjoyment doomed, as is the influence of the moribund potentate, whose days are numbered ? Are they not enjoyed as is wealth by him of whom the demands of equity, the edicts of law, and the superior rights of contestants, require its near transfer?

*   *   *   *   *

To contemplate the history of the last century and a half ; to study the great national movements in the most advanced countries ; to trace their course, their undercurrents, leads one, irresistibly, to the conclusion that the easy communication of ideas, and the consequent dissemination of knowledge and broadening of intelligence, which are noticeable during that period, created a tendency to restrict the undue advantages enjoyed by the few, to extend to the many increased opportunities to rise, to eradicate the glaring contrasts in the positions of men.

This tendency to satisfy, to exhaust, itself, has still a long road to travel; has still much to accomplish. Will it be content with abolishing the semblances of the ancient régime, and re-taining its realities; with withdrawing power from the political king, and transferring it to the financial king; with humiliating the aris-tocracy of birth, and elevating the aristocracy of wealth; with distributing votes among the masses, and concentrating riches in a few hands? Will the tendency to change the old order and to improve the condition of the people, stop there where the old order is most in need of change, there where the people's condition is most in need of improvement?

It is evident—and it is well to bear constantly in mind—that the French Revolution, which did so much to stimulate modern tendencies, was not an independent event, the commencement and end of which can be clearly defined. Nor was it a culminating event. It was intimately linked with occurrences preceding it, and was no less intimately linked with occurrences following it. It was but an episode of a vast revolution, long preparing, and which is going on to this day, the culminating issue of which will be the abolition, not of Monarchy, not of titles of nobility, not of certain forms of government, but the abolition of the state of things—relating to the division of the land, of the wealth, of this world—which found its origin in the ignorance of the mass of men, and which ever-increasing enlightenment is rendering more and more intolerable, less and less likely to endure.

No matter what the apparent cause, or what the immediate effects were, the underlying, the fundamental cause of the explosion of 1789 was economic; and considering that it was but one of many incidents produced, and to be produced, by the same general cause, the ultimate effect must be economic.

Paris—the chief centre from which new knowledge emanated, and also the main centre of the disturbances which led to the outbreak—

was, above all, a monumental city of glaring contrasts. On one side was magnificence, wealth,
and luxury ; on the other was squalor, poverty,
and misery. In one quarter the air resounded
with the whirling of wheels of rich equipages,
in which was enthroned Laziness, driving
through the Avenues of Pleasure; in another,
where the ear was deafened by the turning of
the wheels of Industry, were men, women, and
children, panting, sweating, struggling in the
great race of Life—hopelessly excluded from
the lists wherein leisure and comfort are the
prizes. Here was light in all its glory, and
darkness in all its intensity ; here was a little
world in itself which, unlike the great earth,
revolved not; a world in which there was no
rotation of morning and evening—each hemi-
sphere receiving in turn the rays of the sun ;
each submitting in turn to the shades of night.
One side alone knew sunshine ; the other was
in perpetual gloom.

This it was that helped awaken the spirit of
Revolution which, with drawn sword and flaming torch, wandered over the long-submissive
land ; this it was that caused the proud descend-
ant of *le Roi-Soleil* to be dragged from his
resplendent throne, and sacrificed by his angered

people. Thus, it was thought, the light of day would expand, and penetrate regions it had never reached before. The sunshine the monarch and his favorites once claimed as their due, was diffused indeed—but not in the domain of Darkness. There, as before, was gloom; elsewhere was light—less glaring, because less concentrated, but glaring nevertheless. A king had disappeared; a thousand had taken his place, and were sharing his splendors—a band of merry satraps, each with his festive court, and courtiers, and followers, and many subjects.

Paris was but a symbol of the world. The contrast emphasized there, existed everywhere. The example it held up, the lesson it taught, were universal in their application. The people of the great city felt that things were not as they should be. There was something wrong, they knew not what; there was a remedy, they knew not where. They resorted to revolution; they rose in their might; they wielded their power; and yet, strange magic! they, themselves, were overpowered. Another, and another, revolution; and still the wrong is not righted. What, then, the cause? It cannot be the monarch—he is dethroned, his descendants are banished, his courtiers dispersed, his palaces demolished; his princely personality casts no longer its brilliant light in one direction, its dark shadow in another; yet the people are overshadowed; the *ville lumière* is in darkness.

The kings of France lived, if ever kings did, in stately style. Their palaces were numerous and beautiful; their gardens, dotted with fountains and pavilions, were the smiling abode of Pleasure; the forests, alive with bird and game, resounded with the horn of the royal hunters and the bark of their hounds. At night, what scenes of revelry, of merriment; what gatherings of fair dames and gay cavaliers; what banquets, what feasts, what graceful dances, what entrancing music, giving birth to tender passions —too easily gratified; too easily forgotten!

Accounts of the magnificence of the court of Versailles spread over the world—stimulating imitation on the part of some, awakening envy in the breasts of others; all of which added to the fame and glory of France. Certainly, there was no occasion for the people to object to these things, in themselves. On the contrary, the more lavish the expenditures of their kings; the more courtiers, the more armies, the more ships, the more power they could boast of, the

more reason the people had to be proud, the
more reason they had to exult—for did not the
greatness of their princes reflect greatness on
themselves? But the day came when, far from
finding pride in the lavish expenditures of their
rulers, they felt shame and indignation; for
they were made conscious of the contrast between the gay revellers of the palace and the
weary inhabitants of the huts. A new light
had come to them, and they were, in a measure,
informed as to the cause of this state of things.
Hence they rebelled. They overthrew the
kingly rule, and humiliated the nobles.

This was done, not because the Bourbons had
held supreme sway; not because they had lived
in palaces and were surrounded by an array of
brilliant followers; it was done because, to keep
up the royal state, the nation was impoverished;
it was because the manner of life, the conditions, the surroundings of the kings and the
nobles, considered in their relations to the manner of life, the conditions and surroundings of
the majority of the people, were found to affect
these adversely; it was because the regal splendors and extravagance were maintained in the
face of the poverty, and at the expense, of the
masses.

Nor is it to be supposed that the subjects of the king would have objected if the latter had exercised the power of the most despotic of rulers, provided that power had been exercised to insure them a fair subsistence, and the enjoy-ment of those emoluments they claimed as the due of their toil, and as their reasonable propor-tion of the riches produced by them. Where the people so blind to reason, so indifferent to their welfare, as to hesitate between an Empire with a despot at its head, whose aim is the dis-semination of wealth and its advantages, and a Republic which tolerates a privileged class of citizens who, protected by law, are striving for the monopoly of all that wealth brings? As well expect an intelligent man to prefer an inn where the fare is poor and scanty, but whose sign is the cap of Liberty, to one with a crown and sceptre over the entrance, where a rich feast awaits him.

It is manifest, therefore, that the dismissal of Royalty was not due to purely political causes. Furthermore, it would never have been resorted to, had it not been thought that, under a differ-ent régime, different conditions would have en-sued. How could it be expected that the mere removal of a king, or of a score of kings, could,

in itself, prove advantageous to the people, unless the king himself stood in the way of their
advancement, and unless the new order, which
it was proposed to adopt in lieu of the old one,
aimed at their promotion and welfare? Why
overthrow a government which is accused of
being the cause of the misfortunes of the nation,
unless for the purpose of freeing the nation of
those very misfortunes? Why dethrone a prince
whose extravagance is ruining the country, unless the object be to allow the inhabitants
thereof to apply to themselves that which the
prince wasted?

Under the circumstances, the subversion of
Monarchy, and its eventual substitution by Democracy, was the most insane, the most purpose-
less, the most inconsistent, the most eccentric,
the most incomprehensible, of acts, unless in
doing so the people contemplated benefiting
themselves in the manner alluded to ; nor is it
reasonable to come to any other conclusion than
that—however concealed by artificial and ex-
traneous excitements—the real cause of the
Revolution was economic and not political, and
that whatever political changes were aimed at,
were aimed at to secure economic effects.

These economic effects are still to be realized.
Lulled, at first, into the soothing belief that the
hasty demolition of forms meant the early removal of the cause of their grievances; lured,
later on, by the delusive hope that the fairy-like
development of newly-discovered forces, the expansion of Industry, and the consequent fabulous increase of wealth, might induce Fortune
to cast some of her flowers in their path, the people have seen many years slip by, without any
material change being effected in their position.
But is not this change bound to be brought
about ? Are not the economic effects referred
to already beginning to manifest themselves ?
Are there not indications that the tendency to
restrict the undue advantages of the few, and
increase the opportunities of the many, which
seemed, for a time, to be dying out, is taking
new life, and making itself felt with renewed
force ? Is it not evident that the revolution,
the general revolution, caused by the spread of
Knowledge—and of which the upheavals of the
last century were but incidents—far from being
ended, is still progressing towards its legitimate,
its only, issue ?

Glance over the field—everywhere are signs,
glaring to the observing eye. The restlessness

7

of the masses, the mutterings of discontent, the cries for reform, for change, which are becoming more and more regular, more and more general, in America as well as in Europe, are but forerunners of what is to follow.

In what country, be it a Democracy or a Monarchy, is not uneasiness felt at the progress of what is known as the conflict between Capital and Labor, or what might be better termed, the conflict between Wealth and Poverty? The fact that republics are not exempt from this uneasiness, is proof that they have not solved, any more than have monarchies, the one and all important question affecting the welfare of the governed.

Royalty being overthrown, or subdued, without the desired end being attained; and it being therefore obvious that royalty alone was not the cause of the evil, the people, still having grievances, are turning their attention in another direction. Capital is now threatened; nor is the threat an empty one. The formidable chain of organized labor, binding together powerful bodies of determined men, is not destined to continue merely defensive. Resistance to abuses is inevitably followed, in the course of time, by insistence on rights. Nor should it be forgotten that, independent of organized labor—which constitutes a mightier army than any the world has yet seen—there are legions of silent and inactive protesters against the iniquities of the existing system, who await but the opportunity to make their influence felt. It would be a grievous error to suppose that the element of discontent is by any means fully represented in any of the recognized political parties. The millions of voters in imperial Germany, monarchical Italy, and republican France, who, every election, send an increased number of socialist representatives to the legislative halls of their country, form but a small contingent of those who will, before long, raise their voices against the usurpation of the rights of Intelligence, against the abuses of inheritance, and the long tolerated tyranny of inordinate wealth. Even as matters now stand, is not Berlin—the home of the war-lords of Europe—also the home of the socialist? Though one of the great financial centres of the Continent, do not the avowed enemies of Capital sit as her representatives in the Reichstag? Does not Paris, with her lingering memories of regal splendors, now count among her rulers, men who oppose the despotism of

Wealth no less than the despotism of Princes? And Rome, and Vienna, and London, and the populous cities of the great American Common-wealth, are they not familiar with the turbu-lence which springs from dissatisfaction and the strain in the economic relations of the classes?

Signs—where, indeed, are they not seen? Voices—where, by day or by night, are they not heard? And yet there are those who see not; there are those who hear not.

In the ancient city of hanging gardens, Belshazzar, indulging in high revelry, sur-rounded by satraps, wives, and concubines, was not blind to the writing on the wall. Struck with awe, he commanded the feast to end; he sent for men of lore, to interpret the mystic words; he recognized in them portents of his impending fate. In the Babylons of modern times, Mammon, surrounded by min-ions and courtiers, attended by slaves of form divine, is still feasting in gilded halls. En-trancing are the strains of music, sweet the fragrance of flowers, exhilarating the golden wine which flows from crystal goblets; but he, drunk with pleasure, dazed by the glamour of his environment, sees not the writing on the wall. Yet there it is in flaming letters:

Mene, mene, tekel, upharsin—

Thou art weighed in the balance and art found wanting; thy kingdom awaits division.

*   *   *

Tides in the affairs of nations, once they set in, do not vary from day to day, like those of the ocean. There may be periods of surging tumult or of peaceful calm; there may be flux or reflux; but the movement, whether backward or forward, is destined to follow to its limits the course which the inexorable Fates have traced.

For centuries, the tendency was to reduce to a minimum the rights of the people, and increase to a maximum those of the ruler. One was crushed, the other exalted; one was a trembling subject, the other supreme master. Now the tendency is reversed; the tide is set in the opposite direction. It is in the higher quarters that restrictions are being exacted, while they are being relaxed there where oppression was formerly practised. Those who were exalted, are being lowered—masters no longer, but servants of the State; those who were crushed, are being exalted—subjects no longer, but sovereign people.

The tide which has turned against princes

and nobles, must overtake, in its resistless course, all those who now enjoy undue advantages and privileges. The financial king will have to submit to the alternative presented to the political king, of reduction, or destruction, of his powers; of bowing to the general will, or having his crown removed by other hands than his own. He will have to consent to the elimination of those abuses which he has fostered, and which are the cause of the people's just remonstrance. He will have to accede to a reorganization which will tend to give fair opportunities to all in the contest for the prizes of life. He will have to surrender to others a portion of that which he now monopolizes—the sunshine of this broad, this fair, earth.

If, when pressed by necessity, the people resisted extravagance in one who was, by law, their master, will they tolerate it long in those who are, by law, their equals? If, when but half conscious of the iniquities that weighed upon them, their action was so determined, is it difficult to foresee what they will do when their illusions have vanished; when full knowledge has dawned upon them; when they discover that the tyranny of great wealth is no less oppressive than the tyranny of despots?

And, in imitation of the autocrats—their pre-decessors in the control of this world—are not the plutocrats compassing their own ruin? The ambition to consolidate their power, to increase it, to deprive others of any share therein, and to use it for the exclusive advantage and aggrandizement of themselves and their minions, caused the fall of mighty dynasties. What seemed to be their triumph was, in reality, the forerunner of their downfall. Like that of the setting sun, their glory was greatest as it was about to depart. So, likewise, the reign of Mammon, now at its apogee, is on the verge of its decline. So, likewise, are those who have the greatest interest in maintaining it, bringing about its subversion. They are provoking, stimulating, consolidating, the forces which are antagonistic to their supremacy. They are, in their blindness, hurrying forward the economic revolution which means the collapse of their power, the end of their rule.

The accumulation of wealth in one quarter; its scarcity in another, have disturbed the social balance. Some rise to dizzy heights; others fall to perilous depths. The very foundations of the social structure are being worn out by the consequent friction. Such a state of things prohibits the possibility of equilibrium. It is this lack of equilibrium which threatens to upset society. The policy of accretions in the hands of the few is persisted in, notwithstanding the fact that the number of people to be provided for is continually growing larger. Population is ever on the increase. The majority of the population being poor, the majority of the increase must be poor. This is cumulative in its effects in the same manner as the hoarding of riches is cumulative. Hence, while wealth is being concentrated, the population which is dependent thereon is expanding. Thus, matters, instead of tending toward an adjustment, are daily drifting therefrom. Those who are least in need of wealth are growing wealthier; those who are most in need of it are growing more numerous. The inevitable result is at hand; the civilized world is drifting into two camps; the few, with their opulence, on one side; the many, with their poverty, on the other. Tests of strength are becoming more frequent; skirmishes have ceased to cause wonder. Under such circumstances as these, it requires no prophet to foretell that the mists of the Future, on rising, will reveal emissaries of Peace and Compromise emerging from the ramparts of

Capital, or the world, in turmoil, resounding with the alarm of battle.

The issue must be met; it cannot be averted any more than can thunder when electric clouds clash. Should the pressure not be lessened; should the storm, long gathering, break forth, ruin and devastation will sweep over the land; the social structure, vulnerable in many points —constantly agitated, because unevenly balanced—will not withstand the shock.

In the olden days, when human affairs were in the early stage of development and the mass of men were ignorant, the unevenness of conditions was consistent with the then existing state of things; but the time is at hand when undue preponderance will prove as much an element of disturbance in the economic, as it is in the physical, world; when it will be an offense against laws self-armed with retribution to all infringers thereof. Disturb the equilibrium of the heavenly bodies, and chaos will pervade the universe; the marvellous organization of ages, extending through space, will crumble before the fatal influence of anarchism; all order, all system, all harmony, will vanish.

Can man expect his frail edifice to stand conditions which would cause the mighty fabric of

Nature to fall? Can he hope to defy laws, to resist a force, before which all else must bend?

* * * * *

Two monarchs, whose interests are diametrically opposed, cannot long occupy the same territory; not any more than can fire and water occupy the same space. We are approaching the period when enlightened Democracy and privileged Plutocracy—the Sovereign People and the Majesty of Wealth—will be made to realize the fact that their paths lie apart; that their interests are antagonistic; that they are two powers which cannot, should not, exist under the same head. If Democracy lives, Plutocracy must fall; if Plutocracy lives, Democracy must fall; if Democracy falls, the great civilizations of the West will crumble; the hidden forces which have toiled for centuries will have toiled in vain; cause and effect will be disconnected.

Democracy, in its full, and as yet unfulfilled, sense, implies the supremacy of the people and the predominance of their interests; just as Monarchy, in its full sense, implies the supremacy of the monarch and the predominance of his interests; just as Aristocracy, in its full sense, implies the supremacy of the aristocracy and the predominance of their interests. But though the supremacy of Democracy is recognized, we see the strange spectacle of the interests of Plutocracy being predominant. The first enjoys sovereignty; the second all the fruit of sovereignty.

Nor does the anomaly, which the existing state of things presents, end here. Plutocracy is, beyond contradiction, pursuing a course which is detrimental to the general welfare. Enjoying prerogatives inherited from despotic ages, it has acquired a power dangerous to the State; claiming undue privileges, of an artificial nature, it has infringed on the natural rights of the community; parading itself as of superior origin, it has, in imitation of the favored classes of old, sought to stamp the remainder of mankind as an inferior creation; arrogating to itself the luxuries and pleasures of life, it deems drudgery the lot of all beyond its pale; scheming incessantly for its own aggrandizement, it enlarges the sphere of poverty and consequent discontent; producing moral as well as physical distress, it is awakening in the people a frame of mind similar to that which animated them in 1789, and incited them to rebellion; inciting the people to rebellion, it threatens government itself. Yet, paradoxical as it may appear, the latter, as at present constituted, is powerless to arrest this evil course. Its first, its imperative, duty is to enforce the laws as they now stand. The main purpose of existing laws is to protect property. The bulk of property being in the hands of the minority, it is manifest that laws, and consequently government, are mainly for the benefit of the minority. It is the latter, representing accumulated wealth, who, by their greed and arrogance, are inciting the people to rebellion, and are thus menacing the State; yet the State is compelled to protect and uphold them, and thus become a factor in the revolt against itself.

What power is there, in heaven or on earth, which, if appealed to, could save that which is impelled to take arms against itself, and carries in its system the germ of self-destruction? What genius, however inventive, can devise arguments to defend the consistency of a government which, representing the interests of the majority of the governed, is bound, by law, to sustain the rapacity of the minority? What, with all the good-will conceivable, can be urged in favor of laws which, in their actual form, can offer no relief to great numbers suffering from the association of poverty, the sting of iniquity, and the oppression of a dominant class; and are compelled to gather under their protecting wing that same class which, surfeited with wealth, is striving to acquire more?

How long can the absurdity of this paradox remain obscured to the people? How long can they remain blind to its glaringness? On this will depend the duration of the present incongruous state of things, so offensive to right and reason; on this will depend the fixing of the date when the great, the practical, change will take place; when the two rival monarchs, Plutocracy and Democracy, will part company; the first to wander back among the ruins of Antiquity and Ignorance; the second to step forward and occupy, with undisputed power, the throne which Progress and Enlightenment have prepared for its triumph.

*　　*　　*　　*　　*

Not the least notable feature of the revolution which is progressing; not the least striking evidence of the tendencies of the times, is the transfer of political power from the king and the privileged classes to the nation at large. This power, wielded by the sovereign, was the most visible sign of authority in the land; it towered over and above the multitudes; it impressed the popular eye; it occupied the public thought; it was the subject of public comment.   Hence, when Monarchy fell, it was natural that this power should be inherited by those who were destined to be the successors of kings: the sovereign people.

New causes produce new effects.   Political power in the hands of the masses is a new cause, born of the modern intellectual development, the inevitable effects of which are beginning to be felt, but, as already stated, by no means adequately understood.

Humanity craves for power.   It is, in some form or other, the dominant passion of the race. It is the chosen guide to victory in the universal battle of life.   Man loves it in nearly all its aspects, and seeks it even elsewhere than in himself.   He dives deep into the mysteries of the Unknown, in quest of hidden agencies.   From the domain of Nature he has wrested marvellous forces, which he has made his own and enslaved to his daily purposes.   Nor is he yet satisfied. Stealing fire from the heavens, propulsion from the winds, electricity from the clouds, currents from the earth, are but initial steps in the ambitious course in which, with "Excelsior" for his device, he strives to ascertain, maybe to use, the powers which formed and sustain the universe.

But if man craves for power, he craves it for a purpose; if he seeks it, it is because it is useful to him; it is because it advances his cause, serves his interests, helps improve his condition. This it is which constitutes the might of wealth; this it is which emphasizes the impotency of poverty; this it is which makes all men strive for riches.

Without a purpose, visible or latent, power cannot be said to exist. What, then, is the purpose of political power? To what use will it be put by the people, who are now masters thereof? Let those who believe it to be an idle phrase, a pleasing sound, intended to flatter the ear of the multitude, be undeceived. It is a formidable weapon, the use of which is authorized by law, with which they will go forth, some day, to claim a share of Mother Earth's inheritance.

Princes and privileged classes, when this same power was vested in them, were not loth to use it to their own advantage and advancement. What marvel, then, if its new possessors should imitate their example?

If given the ballot, the masses may be expected, sooner or later, to agitate for a fairer division of the wealth of the land; if given education in conjunction with the ballot, they will surely demand and obtain that division; nay, it is a direct invitation to the many to partake of the royal feast now spread in Mammon's halls.

The mental improvement produced, in recent years, by the education of the masses, must inevitably be followed by a corresponding improvement in their material situation. It is a change of conditions, which calls for a change of laws; it is a turning-point in the transitional affairs of men. This being the case, the purpose of the political power of the people cannot long remain latent; nor can it long be resisted once it asserts itself. Indeed, under Democracies, resistance to this power would be a breach of the first, the supreme, law; with the sovereign nation as the high-offended party, it would be a flagrant case of *lèse-majesté.*

The actual magnitude of the power of steam and electricity was unknown in the first stages of their discovery. In time, study and observation, as well as necessity, revealed the universality of the new forces; their influence began to be felt in every quarter of the globe; their uses became well-nigh unlimited; old methods were abandoned, new ones adopted. Changes, of which the imagination, in its wildest flights, had never dreamed, were visible on all sides. Enemies of innovation were routed; skeptics were ridiculed; critics were silenced. The most far-seeing genius of former ages, revisiting this mundane sphere, would have deemed himself in a land over which the enchanter's wand had passed. The aspect of cities was altered; the country was transformed. Structures, novel in appearance, dotted the plains and reached nearer the sky than the spires of churches, and the trees of the forest. Labor, which formerly required human effort, was performed as though by magic. Highways of steel ran from ocean to ocean, spanning immense continents, regardless of mountains and rivers. Distances which had demanded days to cover, were reached in a few hours. The electric wire encircled the earth, and communication with the remotest points became instantaneous. Time and space were conquered; the world was revolutionized.

And so is it with political power. It is a new force in the hands of the multitude. Its vastness, its possibilities are, as yet, imperfectly appreciated. But the people are not idle ; they are studying, they are observing; above all, they are, by means of education and by force of necessity, becoming familiar with its uses. When these are fully understood and mastered ; when they are put into intelligent operation, there will be a hum in the air to which the ear is at present unaccustomed ; there will be innovations which conservatism now opposes with steadfast stubbornness, which skeptics now pronounce impracticable, which critics now ridicule and condemn as subversive; we shall witness in the economic world a revolution no less remarkable—and in time, no less beneficial—than that produced in the industrial world by the agency of steam and electricity.

CHAPTER IX.

WHAT COURSE SHALL ENLIGHTENED DEMOCRACY FOLLOW?

AS the people become more enlightened, indications of the eventual disappearance of the conditions which sprung from ignorance multiply. These indications have, in recent times, increased to such an extent, and assumed such a definite aspect, that the nature of the movement they portend can no longer be ignored. Democracy—being gradually instructed and fully equipped—is now a moving, living, thinking force, whose influence is universally felt, and whose power must become the dominant power—not in name merely, but in fact. This supremacy will be used to advance the interests of those who enjoy it; it will, necessarily, call for a readjustment of the affairs of this world on a basis consistent with the new condition of things, and which will differ materially from that which prevailed when the people were densely ignorant, and which prevails, in its main features, to this day.

What, then, shall be the basis of the new arrangement?   Since a change is inevitable, in what shall the change consist?

It is a common impulse to oscillate from one extreme to the other.   The momentum which propels us, having exhausted itself in one direction, becomes instrumental in propelling us in the opposite direction.   We swing from love to hatred, from calmness to anger, from hope to despair, without stopping, at so important a juncture, to consult wisdom, which would, beyond peradventure, urge him who suffers the pangs of unrequited love, to avoid further misery and seek consolation in paying court to indifference ; would whisper to him whose calmness has been provoked to the point of anger, that tempered indignation will disarm his adversary quicker than a surrender to passion ; would direct deceived hope from the sombre path of despair, and guide it to the peaceful abode of resignation.

If then, in personal matters, wisdom raises a warning finger to impulse, how much more impressive must be its warning in matters which concern the race ?

Those who, protesting against the abuses of the existing system, advocate its annihilation, are of the opinion that we should swing—some say slowly, others swiftly—from the absolutism of capital to absolute socialism. It is in this direction they are endeavoring to guide Democracy when, realizing its power, it shall have overthrown Plutocracy and assumed supreme control.

Ere adopting this course, it were well to pause. The fear is lest Democracy, in completely subverting the existing system, should damage its own cause. Victories there are which might prove more disastrous than defeats. Disastrous, indeed, would be the victory which would consist in having demolished the present social structure, without having prepared a better one for the protection of the race; futile would be the efforts to improve man's estate, if, in the attempt to do so, he is to be considered—not as he is, with his foibles, his propensities, his ambitious, but as he might be—an ideal being, a creature of the imagination.

To him who can take wings and soar beyond the realms of prejudice and self-interest; to him who can look down on humanity as being swayed by the highest and purest motives; to him who is convinced that the proclamation to

man of the moral and the physical law, will
ensure the strict observance of those laws ; to
him, absolute socialism is not only the most perfect and most equitable of systems devised by
mortal, but also the most practicable. Indeed,
who can fail to accord it praise, and concede to
its devisers and followers honesty of purpose
and sincere love of mankind ?

The conception of socialism is the natural
outgrowth of the evils of capitalism—which
evils it proposes to eradicate. While the existing system betrays many inconsistencies, in-
justices, and imperfections, socialism aims at
universal consistency, universal justice, universal perfection. Surely, no purpose could be
higher, nobler, than this. But so beautiful, so
elevated, is the conception of absolute socialism,
that it partakes of the ideal, and one is tempted ·
to question its applicability to real men, living
in a real world. It is to be feared that its per-
manent adoption would imply less of a social,
than a moral, revolution, and that man's nature
would have to undergo changes far more difficult to obtain than any to which his institutions
would have to submit.

Absolute socialism, though eminently just in
principle, is to be condemned because, in prac-

tice, it would, by destroying the stimulus to energy and genius, prove detrimental to the race. Plutocracy, which is virtually supreme to-day, is to be no less condemned; for it is not only not just, but is nearly as detrimental to the race at large as absolute socialism would be, if adopted; and, moreover, it is in direct opposition to the spirit of Democracy, whose interests are destined to become paramount.

What, then, is to be done? On one side we have a system which, so long as it is burdened with its iniquitous favoritism, should not, and cannot endure; on the other, a proposed, and the only seriously proposed, substitute, which, while claiming to favor all, would prove ruinous to some and beneficial to none. One is destined to fall by the weight of its own defects; the other cannot be raised owing to the frail foun- dation on which it would rest.

To attain its end, to fulfil its mission, is it necessary for Democracy to go to extremes, and completely subvert the actual order? Should it, casting aside its proud claim to enlighten- ment, disregard the admonitions of wisdom, and follow its blind impulses? However superficial in its superstructure, the existing system is not without solidity in its foundation. It is not faulty in its conception, but in its execution; not in its principles, but in their application. Should it perish, should it be condemned in its entirety, because certain abuses—great and reprehensible, it is true—have invaded its sphere? Should emulation, which might be made to encourage industry, and keep in play the energies which are the mainspring of the race, be cast aside as detrimental to mankind, because a few have overstepped the equitable lines of competition, and arrogated to themselves more and richer prizes than the general welfare would suggest, or than justice should tolerate? Should we sacrifice benefits which are within reach, to grasp blindly at that which our better sense tells us is undesirable and, as we are at present constituted, unattainable, if it were desirable? Shall we resort to a course of demolition and devastation, when by altering or by pruning we can attain the desired end? Shall we forego the actual order and forfeit all its possible advantages, or do away with its glaring contrasts and excessive favoritism—which are its main, if not its sole, defects—and thus make it consistent with the aims, the spirit, of enlightened Democracy? Shall we take steps, and decisive steps, to arrest the greed of the few

and mitigate the wants of the many ; to curtail
the privileges of some and recognize the rights
of others ?   Shall we, in one word, attempt
what is possible, because in the realms of Reality ; or venture on the impossible, in the alluring but impenetrable fields of Idealism ?

*   *   *   *   *

The basis of the new arrangement should be
the one on which true, and not the present
fictitious, Democracy rests; the change to be
wrought should consist in putting into practice
those popular principles, so loudly vaunted,
which now exist only in theory.

True Democracy does not necessarily imply
government by the people ; but it does emphatically imply government for the people.   It
requires that there shall be no class enjoying
undue privileges, unearned advantages, over
others.   It demands the enforcement of laws having for object the welfare of the greatest possible
number of those living under that government.

In the fulfilment of this purpose, every ob-
stacle should be removed, every precaution
should be taken.   No interference, from whatsoever quarter, should be tolerated ; no personal
interests, however cherished, should be permitted to stand in the way of general interests;

no claims, however pressing, should be allowed which come in conflict with the public weal.

A strong executive, armed with full authority, and with imposing power to enforce that authority, is by no means foreign to the democratic idea. Once laws—clearly stated—aiming to benefit the nation at large, to promote their welfare and protect their interests, have received the people's sanction, and are the admitted expression of their will, no executive can be too strong to enforce that will. His powers, his functions, being strictly limited to this, he becomes the personification of the people; his voice becomes their voice; his strong arm becomes their arm; his majesty becomes their majesty.

Since it is the people as a whole, and not a class, who are to derive the main benefit under democratic rule, the question arises, Wherein, mainly, are the people to be benefited? The manifest answer to this question is that they can best be benefited by having within reach all the means available to improve their condition. This is not only the chief end they are striving to attain, but it is in this respect that their circumstances differ mainly from those of the existing privileged classes. Indeed, the improvement of their condition is the most general and at the same time the most reasonable and legitimate of all the desires of civilized men. It is the incentive which has exercised the widest influence on the race; the one which, more than all others, has hastened the turning of the wheels of progress, stimulated the spirit of invention, caused the fields of science to be explored, made grateful the task of study and easy the effort of labor. It is this desire, in some form or other, which underlies every action, suggests every undertaking. The ultimate object of industry, of commerce, of the arts and the sciences, is the production, the handling, the perfectionment or discovery of means to render our sojourn on this globe as agreeable as possible. The millions of hands who cultivate the soil and toil in factories; the army of miners who penetrate the bowels of the earth in search of its treasures; the daring men who plunge into the depths of the ocean to bring forth the coveted pearls; youth and age bending over desks; authors burning the midnight oil; artists laboring in their studios, scientists in their laboratories, statisticians in their libraries, multitudes in their garrets—all are animated by the hope of improving their condition.

What, then, are the requirements of a people in the furtherance of this commendable ambition? Those which are, perhaps, the most generally referred to, are industry and education—without which, certainly, no nation could progress. It is obvious, however, that in established communities, at least, these two, alone, cannot always accomplish the desired end; since, as we have seen, the masses who are most industrious, partake of conditions far less desirable than those of certain classes who boast of their indolence; and there are men of superior mental training whose positions are to be pitied, while others, with inferior or purely ornamental educations, occupy the most enviable positions in life.

Inasmuch as a large portion of the population, with education and industry, are not only unable to better their situation, but have to struggle constantly to maintain existence, while a small portion, who are strangers to toil and to whom education is a mere adornment, partake of conditions which, from a material standpoint, it would be difficult to better, it is manifest that the latter have at their disposal something which the former have not; something, the possession of which implies an enormous advantage in promoting the improvement of one's condition, since it, alone, can bring about results which industry and education combined often strive vainly to attain. This something, so marvel-lously effective in its operation, so all-sufficient to its possessors, is wealth. This, in the complex adjustments of our social organism, is the most potent factor in bringing about an amelioration of the circumstances of individuals; for, as al-ready stated, it matters not under what form of government—constitutional or despotic, monar-chical or republican—man lives, his environment is likely to be little affected thereby; whether he be Jew or Gentile, Protestant or Catholic, does not determine what advantages he shall enjoy; whether he has political rights or not, does not, *per se*, improve his condition in life; but whether he be poor or rich does most ma-terially affect his condition. He may change his divinities, or his rulers, or his opinions, and these will in no wise change his station; but let the size of his purse be changed one way or the other and lo! he and his surroundings are immediately altered, and the world is to him as a new world; his powers, his actions, his de-sires are amplified or restricted; he appears as a god amongst men, or as a menial amongst gods. So manifest, indeed, is the superiority which wealth gives its possessor; so great is the contrast between the opulent and the poor class, that there is some excuse for the impression which prevails among certain members of the former, that they are of a race superior to the latter.

To the child of Fortune is given the golden key which opens to him the wide world. He is a free man—free to do what fancy suggests; free to wander where pleasure calls him. He is enabled to secure all physical and all mental enjoyments and attainments. Circumstance forces him into a superior position—too seldom appreciated, too often abused!—the occupancy of which calls for little praise; for, with the means at his command, it would be difficult not to occupy it, even when not inherited. Respect, consideration, distinction, yes—and love, are within his easy reach. Abundance, superfluity, attend him on every side. He is given of all things till overtaken by satiety. Leisure and luxury, so craved for by many, to him become monotonous. He grows weary of the indulgence of those pleasures of which the multitudes never taste.

The poor man, on the contrary, though he hears much of sweet liberty, is a slave to adverse

circumstance. His hands are chained, his movements circumscribed, his wishes ungratified.
He is, at times, made to feel the stinging lash
of contempt, and bear the haughty treatment of
domineering masters. He searches, often in vain,
for an outlet for whatever reserve of effort,
energy, and ambition he may possess. Intelligent, educated, may be refined and cultured, yet
unable, through lack of capital, to work for
himself, he is not always allowed the privilege
of working for others. He gazes at this immense earth, and yet cannot lay claim to a single
inch thereof. He lingers at the threshold of
the highways of the world and, not having the
wherewith to pay toll, finds the gates closed to
him. In his case, the struggle is less to develop
and perfect latent mental powers, than to sustain material existence. He is forced into an
inferior position; nor should any odium be attached to him on this account, for there are
innumerable and often insurmountable obstacles
in the way of his rising. No matter what his
capacity and ability, the occasion to use these
being denied him, he must walk his lowly path.
Birth and circumstance, which combine in favor
of his affluent rival, are allied against him, and
compel him to strive for that which is freely

proffered the other. Yet both are human, both draw life from the same source, both dwell under the same azure roof; both may be equally favored by the hand of nature; but, surely, both have not been equally favored by the laws of man.

The advantages which the few who control great wealth have over those who own little or none, are too evident to require being elaborately dwelt upon. The opportunities which riches offer in the acquiring of knowledge, of culture and refinement, as well as the comforts and luxuries of life, are sufficient proof that they are powerful instruments in improving, not only our mental, but our material, condition.

Under existing arrangements, wealth is the embodiment of power. Without it, all the crowns and sceptres of the earth would be mere baubles. Its possession or non-possession decides whether one's position shall be high or low, considered or despised; it determines whether our bodies shall enjoy plenty or suffer want; whether our minds shall know peace or endure strife; it ordains whether our sojourn on this planet is to be one of pleasure or of misery, one of toil or of leisure; it regulates the quantity and the quality of those things desirable, or necessary, one may acquire ; it prescribes how much liberty one may claim ; how much of that indefinite thing, called Time, one may call his own ; in fact, it decides how much of this world, and that which it contains, one may possess.

Since, then, wealth can accomplish so much ; since the extent of its ownership affects the condition, the position, the happiness of every individual of a nation ; since it is the admitted means of satisfying man's most natural, most reasonable, most legitimate, desire—that of improving himself and embellishing his environment—it is manifest that democratic rule, aiming to benefit the people at large, far from allowing a class to monopolize wealth, should devise means to secure its distribution among the greatest possible number, consistent with the general good.

*   *   *   *   *

Whatever else may be said of this earth, she is generous in her resources, and responsive to the needs of those who live thereon. She has immeasurable wealth which she yields liberally to man's labor. For untold past centuries she has sent forth fruit for the nourishment of her children, and seems disposed to do so for untold centuries to come. She is certainly an earth of

9

plenty; nay, we have known periods when man, pressing his suit for her favors, received more than he could well dispose of. Nor has the race been negligent in utilizing the materials which nature seemed to hold in reserve for their benefit. In every quarter of the globe is found evidence of the stupendous work accomplished by man—not only to sustain life; not only to secure the useful, but the beautiful. In this task his genius has contrived to lend assistance to his hand; it has helped increase a thousand-fold the power of production, and as a result we see an increase of a thousand-fold in the wealth of the world.

But notwithstanding the bounteousness of nature and the never-slacking labor of man; notwithstanding the almost fairy-like assistance which newly-discovered forces and appliances lend to human efforts; notwithstanding the facility with which new riches are produced, and their almost incredible growth during the past century, the majority of the people are still poor, and many of these are in actual want. And this is due, to a very considerable extent, to the gross inequality in the division of wealth. The latter is absorbed by the few, hence it cannot be applied as a means to improve the condition of the many. Whatever increase there is in productive power; whatever increase there is in riches; whatever advantage is drawn from the sciences, the arts—from progress in any form—the minority derive the main benefit thereof.

Labor-saving machinery, which implies that humanity, as a whole, will have to labor less, should, one might think, be welcome to all humanity. As a matter of fact, it is really welcome to very few; and these few, odd as it may appear, are not workers; therefore the labor-saving machine does not reduce their work. But it is welcome to them because it increases their revenue; because they can secure from one machine results it once required many hands to secure.

Multitudes of men look upon many modern inventions as their worst enemies, for they deprive them of the opportunity to labor, and by labor alone can they live. Thus, that which should cause the whole of mankind to rejoice, causes large numbers to despond; that which should be hailed by them as a blessing, is considered as a curse!

So long as laws fail to prohibit the unreasonable and unjust inequality in the division of the goods of this earth, they constitute a cause which must have the inevitable effect of attracting riches toward the rich, and repelling them from the poor. This, under existing economic conditions, is as certain to occur as, under existing physical conditions, certain bodies are attracted to others, while others are repelled. Material progress might advance by leaps and by bounds, and wealth accumulate to a fabulous degree; the sands of our shores might be turned to grains of gold; the mountains might be transformed into solid masses of iridium; but while the laws stand as they now stand, progress and wealth will continue to follow the fixed channel traced for them, and increase the beauty, luxuriance, and delights of the oasis of the favored band, while leaving the arid plains, whereon the multitudes dwell, as desolate and unattractive as formerly. For this is the natural result of prevailing laws, and, these laws enforced, their effect cannot be avoided.

Thus, while men are associated in a social body, and are ruled by laws theoretically for the benefit of all, the fact is that the majority of men, thus associated, are the recipients of the fewest benefits. Society, instead of being based, as is often claimed, on the principle that

its working should redound to the advantage
of the greatest possible number, and that the
interests of a portion thereof should not be
paramount to the interests of the whole, is
based, practically, on the principle that its
working should redound to the advantage of
the smallest number, and that the interests of
the whole are insignificant as compared with
those of a portion thereof. The entire spirit
of society—its customs, laws, government—is
tainted with this purpose. The proof of this
lies in the fact that the majority of the members of the social body are kept in a state of
constant activity, so as to sustain the minority
in a state of constant leisure; they are kept in
a state bordering on misery and want, so as
to sustain the few in a state of luxury and
abundance.

And this is termed a competitive system, and
is praised as such; whereas, be it observed, the
principal defect of the system, the defect from
which flows all the evils and abuses which render it vulnerable, is that, no restriction being
placed on the greed and selfishness of men, a
small number of these have been allowed to
acquire a monopoly of the most valuable prizes
of life; and owing to no limit being placed on

inheritance, the enjoyment of these prizes is, to a great extent, excluded from competition for all time. This has caused society to be divided into two classes: one, by far the more numerous and more powerful, composed of poor men who, to maintain themselves, are compelled to compete with each other for work; the other, numerically weak, composed of rich men who, to amuse themselves and gratify their vanity, first crush those who interfere with their game, and then proceed to compete with each other for greater wealth.

As operated at present, the system is, in its most serious aspect—that is, the maintenance of life—competitive for the poor, not for the rich. The latter form a class apart, and belong to a system which, in its nature and require-ments, is the reverse of competitive. Having all, and more, than they need, they are not forced to enter the lists of the battle of life; the mandate which went forth from the gates of Eden, to the human race, does not apply to them; they toil not by the sweat of their brow, yet have they, in abundance, of bread and of fruit, of the good and the fair things of this earth. Not only are they guaranteed protec-tion in the enjoyment of their possessions, but, owing to partial and over-indulgent laws, their offspring, and theirs, whether worthy or not, are made to inherit their wealth, their station in life, and all the benefits these insure.

It might be thought that, in a world where the majority of its inhabitants have to struggle for bare subsistence, these favored mortals would be satisfied with a condition of things which, exempting them from the burden of surrounding hardships, raises them to an exalted situation from which, as demi-gods, they can look down on the masses of suffering humanity. Not so, however. Though there is no necessity for them to enter the already overcrowded field of competition, there are many who enter there nevertheless; and they enter it armed with every advantage. The wealth they control decides, in advance, the contest in their favor; equipped from head to foot, they push aside and overwhelm those whose main strength is required to keep body and soul together. Moreover, they have contrived, by artful manœuvring, to draw all the glory and profits, while leaving to subordinates all the worry and fatigue, of their vast undertakings.

Into such a state has the existing system fallen, that many of those who, by force of circumstances, are impelled to enter the field of competition, are practically shut out; whereas those who have every incentive to withdraw, remain therein, animated by a spirit of greed, the result of which cannot fail to be disastrous to their fellow-creatures. We see the many laboring much, and securing in return little or nothing beyond subsistence; we see the few laboring little, or not at all, and securing nearly everything men contend for. The majority of the members of the social organization, which is supposed to advance the interests of all, are compelled to devote their lives, their energies, to the advancement of the interests of the minority.

It is not religious, dynastic, or political grievances, but the unfair division of wealth and the unfair competition for wealth, which enlightenment is making clear to all, which have called into existence the modern subversive tendencies; it is the contemplation of a few men burdened with riches, when millions are suffering from poverty; it is the accumulation for the benefit of a small number of that which should be made to benefit large numbers; it is the undue inequality between the classes; it is the defect in our constitutions which allows the greed for

gold to have unlimited sway, which has engen-
dered the opposition to the existing system, and
brought forth cries for its destruction ; it is
these which, driving the people to extremes,
have given birth to anarchism, communism, socialism, and the spirit of discontent and restlessness, which is the spirit of the age ; and it is
these which must be done away with, if our institutions are to be saved and social order pre-
served ; it is in these that enlightened Democracy
must bring about a change in the fulfilment of
its duty, its mission.

CHAPTER X.

THE PRINCIPLE OF REWARDS.

I F it is certain that wealth is essential to improve man's condition, it is no less certain
that unless man produce and maintain it, no
other power in the universe will do so.

Wealth does not spring from nothing; nor
does it maintain itself. Now man is, by nature,
sluggish; he requires a stimulus to urge him to
action, to exert himself. If activity be not encouraged, indolence will prevail; if indolence
prevail, not only will new wealth not be created,
but that which already exists will gradually
vanish, and the race will inevitably fall back to
that stage where subsistence would be their
only aim.

It would, therefore, be a task, as superfluous
as it would be inconsequent, to attempt the dis-
semination of wealth without providing, at the
same time, for its production and maintenance.

While the accumulation of riches in the hands
of the few, being detrimental to the welfare of

the many, is essentially undemocratic; while it
is an impediment to general progress and is antagonistic to the spirit of the times; while no
more serious misfortune could befall a nation—
especially if it be one whose intellectual condition is such as to justify the expectation of its
attaining a higher development—than that its
resources should be monopolized by a small
class, to the exclusion of the mass of the people; while no greater danger could face a government, and threaten its legitimate power, than
that of a grasping Plutocracy whose aim is, and
always will be, to make its own interests paramount to all others; while this, and much
more, may be urged against the possession of
inordinate wealth, it by no means follows that
the possession of all wealth should be condemned
as pernicious to the general welfare. As well
denounce the use of food because its abuse calls
for our reprobation. Eating is beneficial; glut-
tony is injurious; but is eating to be discoun-
tenanced because some men are gluttons? And
is all ownership of wealth to be condemned
because a few men own excessive wealth?

If a too great disparity in the possession of
the good and the fair things of this earth is
dangerous, and is to be avoided, it is no less true

that a too great equality would prove no less dangerous, and no less iniquitous. Equality in the enjoyment of wealth, to be consistent, to be just, should be the result of equality in the production of wealth. This, for many reasons, is manifestly impossible. Some men have considerable capacity, mental and physical, for labor; others have little or none. If it were decreed that all should share alike in the possession of the general wealth, those of superior ability might secure greater results, and yet enjoy no greater benefits, than those of inferior ability. This, far from encouraging them to exert themselves, would have the contrary effect. Moreover, all participating equally, many would be tempted to give way to their natural inclinations, and shirk work which is repulsive to them. A state of things more iniquitous, and more disastrous to the general welfare, could not be conceived. The effect upon the production of wealth, and the consequent effect upon the condition of the people, is easy to foresee. Retrogression and decay would be unavoidable.

The acquiring of riches, within certain bounds, could, on the contrary, be made to serve a most beneficial purpose; it could, in its particular line, perform a function no less vital to the social body than that which nutrition renders the individual body; it could be made to act as a stimulus to human energies, and keep alive those forces which are essential to man if he is to pursue a forward course. In other words, if that which is most to be dreaded in respect to the future of the race, is to be fought; if that which is most to be desired, is to be encouraged, wealth should be reserved as a precious prize which, while its contest would be open to all, none could claim who had not proved himself worthy of its possession. The advantages it secures, and the opportunities it offers for the gratification of the desire to ameliorate one's condition, are sufficient guarantee that the fullest mental and physical efforts of mankind would be exerted in its acquirement.

No matter what may be said against the existing system—and the preceding pages have not been devoted to the singing of its praises—it has one redeeming feature, and one which, so long as man is constituted as he is to-day, will have to be the pivotal point in any social adjustment which is destined to last. This cardinal feature is the principle of rewards—of admitting those who have exerted or distinguished themselves above all others, to the enjoyment of certain advantages, both as a recognition of their services and as an incentive for others to follow their example. Indeed, so closely allied is this principle to civilized man's desire to improve his condition, that what was said of the one may well be said of the other. Whatever is recorded as progress; whatever advance has been made in the development of intelligence, in the expansion of knowledge, in the application of energy, in the growth of industry, in the perfectionment of the arts and sciences, can be traced to the system of rewards —or, rather, we are constrained to say, to the system which admitted of the hope of reward; of the prospect of improving one's circumstances, one's condition in life. This hope, though seldom realized beyond a certain sphere; though, to the multitudes, distant like the heavenly stars, yet served as a beacon light to direct mankind in the gloomy paths of labor, in the accomplishment of arduous tasks, in the fulfilment of high ambitions. It was the unseen, and hence deemed mystic, agent, which gradually overcame the barriers of primitive ignorance and barbarism, and forced ajar the gates leading to the glories of modern enlightenment and civilization. It gave birth to, and kept alive, the energies, the genius, of the race; it raised man above the beast, and distinguishes him, above all else, from the beast; nay—so great, so far-reaching is its influence—has it not opened to him a vista, entrancing, alluring, which leads from mortality on earth to immortality in the empyrean realms above?

Withdraw the prospect of recompense, and the great motive power of the civilized world will be annihilated; the incentive to physical energy, the spring of mental activity, will be destroyed; the hum of human progress will be silenced; industry will slumber never to wake again; effort, except to subsist, will be synonymous with folly, and ambition as sterile as the chasing of rainbows; a gloom, unrelieved by the faintest, the most distant, glimmer of light, will pervade the universe.

So universal is the hope of reward, so thoroughly is it an integral portion of our being, that though it plays an all-important rôle in our destinies, we are, for the most part, as unconscious of its existence as we are of some of the vital parts of our body, without which, however, life would be impossible. But though many may be unconscious of its existence, none is free from its influence, none can escape its talismanic power.

The little ribbon, the prize, the medal, the wreath of laurel, the diploma, the honorable mention, stimulate the youth to strive for the first place, when, without these, he might follow his natural bent, and give way to indolence. Later, he is animated by the thought of the material good he might eventually derive from his studies. When man's estate is reached, what is it sustains him in the struggle of life ; what is it incites him to labor, to the acquirement of knowledge and experience, to perseverance in the face of obstacles, but the hope of reward, for himself or for those to whom he is attached ? In the shop, in the factory, in the counting-house, in the fields, in the mines, in the laboratory, in the studio, in the world of letters, in the sphere of diplomacy—everywhere—in the civil service, in the army, in the navy—what stimulates attention to details, to duty, to good and effective work, to improvements, save the hope of recognition, of promotion, and may be the winning of one of the prizes of life ?

The greatest of all religions—that one which has swayed the more civilized nations of the earth for nearly twenty centuries—is based on the principle of reward and punishment. And it is questionable whether any creed, in any clime, or with any people, could endure long, unless this principle were held up as an incentive to good and a moderator to evil. If, then, virtue, the peaceful charm of which we have all experienced, is not sufficiently its own reward, how can it be averred that labor, the hardships of which most of us are familiar with, can be its own recompense?

Undoubtedly there are some who, in their thoughts and actions, are uninfluenced by any ulterior considerations; who love and practise virtue for virtue's sake; but these are rare; and social institutions are organized not for the exceptions, but for the generality of mankind; just as prohibitory laws are enacted, not for those who are naturally inclined to good, but for those who are, or might be, disposed to evil. And as in the moral world, not only has vice to be restrained, but virtue has to be stimulated; so, in the physical world, not only has indolence to be combated, but industry has to be encouraged, by the expectancy of reward.

* * * * *

Owing to the peculiar and unique advantages it affords, and which have already been dwelt upon, wealth is almost universally recognized as the chief reward for which genius, industry, and ability contend.   Under existing conditions, however, wealth is held to such a considerable extent by a small number, that there is little or none left to be awarded to the many other con-testants for its possession.   Moreover, as has been seen, this small number occupy such a vantage ground in the field of competition, that they are virtually masters of the situation, and the majority of men, no matter how intelligent and industrious they may be, far from being able to appear as equally equipped rivals, must, on the contrary, submit to being subordinates or dependents—and this with little hope of ever being anything else.

Thus while the principle of rewards is recog-nized under the actual order of things, its equi-table application is a rare occurrence. It exceeds the bounds of all reason in some instances, and does not approach even the limits of common justice in others.   There are a few favored mortals who enjoy the princely rewards earned by the energy and abilities of ancestors who lived centuries ago, while there are many who possess unusual ability and exert untiring en-ergy, and yet are denied the most trivial requital.

Some are allowed numerous mansions and parks, large retinues of servants and assistants, horses, carriages, and yachts, and a revenue which permits them to secure all the comforts, all the luxuries, all the pleasures this world can afford; while others, whose mental and physical capacities may be equal, or superior, deem themselves fortunate, as things go, in the occupancy of a single room, and in being able to procure the mere necessaries of life. In other words, it is a principle which is flagrantly abused and frequently ignored; it is distorted to such an extent that it is scarcely recognizable; it is considered in some rare cases, overlooked in many, and in all, is applied regardless of equity, expediency, or actual merit, and, worse still, with a total disregard of the rights or claims of other contestants. Leaving out the cases where inheritance comes into play, and where, of course, it is practically overlooked, it operates as does the *roulette*, haphazard, stopping here and there by chance; awarding fabulous sums to some, and sending others off with nothing.

This proceeding may be admirable in connection with a game of chance; it is lamentable in connection with the application of a principle

—a sacred principle—on which rests the welfare of the human race.

It is the persistent misapplication of this principle which is the most serious charge which can be brought against the existing sys- tem. It is against the abuse of this principle— on the observance of which the happiness and progress of a people depend, to a great extent —that modern Democracy is called upon to enter a solemn, a persistent, an effective pro- test.

Once we fairly realize what wealth is—what it can bring to man, what it can accomplish for him—we cannot escape the conviction that its unfair division, and the unfair competition for its possession, is the greatest injustice which can be inflicted on a nation, and one which it is im- possible to associate with an enlightened people having the power to remedy it.

We have seen that the race's sojourn on this earth is conditional on the performance of cer- tain labor; we have seen that food, raiment, and shelter can only be obtained and maintained by constant toil and application; and that, with- out these, mankind would become extinct, or be reduced to a condition similar to that of the savage tribes who dwell in huts, use skins as garments, and sustain themselves on roots, herbs, and the animals and birds of the field and forest. In the earlier periods, mere subsistence was considered, and accepted, as sufficient reward for the performance of labor; indeed, in our time, it is so considered by the ignorant, as it is by the beasts of burden. But lo! man awakens, and, by the light of intelligence, he beholds that this is a beautiful world—a vast, a prolific, a luxuriant world; he realizes that there is more than mere subsistence to strive for; he becomes conscious of greater comforts, of sweeter pleasures, of broader action, of higher planes, of a more perfect mental development, of a deeper joy of living; and he finds that these, and not mere existence, are the prizes to be sought, to be fought for. Though he enjoys them not, he feels the capacity to enjoy them; nay, he has a secret sentiment that he has a right to share in them ; and as, notwithstanding his efforts, his abilities, his aspirations, they seem to be beyond his reach, he uses his intelligence, newly awakened, to inquire into the manner of their awarding. They are prizes, hence they must be rewards. Rewards for what? Inevitable inquiry—yet fatal to those who have long held the unearned monopoly of prizes; fatal inquiry to those who display an accumulation of prizes in the presence of the weary legions who deserve many, but have been denied any!

In days of ignorance, in days of tyranny, the awarding of prizes may have been left to the hand of favoritism; in days of ignorance, in days of tyranny, the advantages of life may have been heaped blindly on a few, regardless of merit, virtue, or valor; regardless of equity, expediency, or policy; regardless of the rights of others; but in an age of enlightenment, in an age of popular government, favoritism should make way for impartiality; the competition of prizes should be free; the awarding of prizes should be just; or, at least, they should be so distributed that an unwarranted accumulation of them in one quarter, to the evident detriment of another, would be impossible.

This, as regards the welfare and progress of the people, should be the chief aim of Democracy. It should strive to stimulate the activities, mental and physical, of the race; it should promote the production of wealth, the advancement in the arts, the sciences, the letters; it should devise means to embellish the world; it should encourage the spirit of invention, of

improvement in the mode of living, of perfectionment in every branch ; it should raise the
standard of ambition, of conduct, of duty ; it
should guide man to better, nobler, aims—to a
broader, higher, life ; and, since heaven is offered
as a reward for virtue, how better can this
higher state on earth be reached, than by stimulating its attainment by an equitable system
of terrestrial rewards, and giving all an equal
opportunity to secure the crown of recompense
—the prize of perseverance, industry, and
genius ?

If the system of rewards, as practised at present, with all its defects and abuses, with its
unfair working and obnoxious application, has
succeeded in doing so much to promote progress, and advance the welfare of humanity ;
what might it not accomplish in the same line,
if freed from these defects and abuses, if prop-
erly, equitably, applied ?

If the vast accumulations of wealth were set
free from the narrow channel in which they are
at present confined ; if they were released and
offered to the world as compensation for actual
energy, actual industry, actual genius, all the
dormant faculties of the race would be awakened, all the latent powers would come into

play; there would be an activity, a movement, a revival—both of body and of mind—such as has never before been witnessed. The principle of emulation, of reward, established on a legitimate, consistent basis, would produce results which would brush aside the criticism of scoffers and the sneers of sceptics; it would silence its now clamorous enemies; it would appeal to the reason, to the sense of justice, of all men.

CHAPTER XI.

THE NECESSITY OF RESTRICTION.

A MORE general and equitable distribution of the wealth of the nation, implies restriction in its possession, and necessarily calls for a disturbance of that ownership which has been described as exorbitant, and as antagonistic to the public weal.

The precedent for this is duly established. Its authenticity is unquestioned, its prominence overshadowing. In regulating and curtailing the prerogatives of kings and the privileges of nobles, the ground was merely broken for regulating and curtailing those of the opulent class. The distribution of the economic power now controlled by this class, is as essential to satisfy the economic rights of the people, as was the distribution of political power, once monopolized by the sovereign and the lords, to satisfy their political rights. In fact, the enjoyment of the latter is, if anything, less consistent with the purposes of Democracy—which should aim to benefit the greatest possible number—than the enjoyment of the former.

Political power, disseminated, loses much of its efficiency ; whereas wealth, concentrated, retains all its efficiency. In one instance, fragments of what was once a puissant unit, are scattered liberally among the people, and are, in consequence, rendered worthless, unless the greater portion of them can be reunited, and thus applied as a means to an end; in the other instance, riches, whose potency is apparent, and whose possession, to a certain extent, is essential to one's welfare, are allowed to accumulate in the hands of a few.

What do the much vaunted political rights, as they are now used, amount to with the majority of those who enjoy them? There are many who would exchange them for a loaf of bread ; there are thousands who, when the occasion presents itself, sell them for a piece of silver ; and there are not a few who are so little impressed with their value, that they seldom, if ever, exercise them.

Political rights, like any other rights, are valuable in proportion to their power to maintain one in the enjoyment of something already possessed, or to secure something desired but not yet possessed. If every poor man in the country were given one hundred votes, while every rich man were deprived of any voice whatever in government, but with the understanding that he was to be left in absolute possession of his millions, which would be the more privileged, which would be the more deserving of envy—the citizen with his hundred votes, or the citizen with his hundred thousand a year? The rich man would not begrudge the poor one all the political rights, all the political honors, which might be showered upon him, provided their financial positions remained unchanged. And for excellent reasons. Who would exchange material advantages for empty honors? Who would not forego titles for the substantial pleasures of life? Who would cling to that which, under the circumstances named, could bring nothing, in preference to that which could command all things?

One thing is clear. The successful movement, above referred to, against the monopoly by a few of political and other privileges and advantages, was a preliminary step towards the fuller recognition and the broader application of the doctrine—the justice of which is universally conceded—that personal interests, even

those of kings and nobles, should be subordinate
to general interests.

From time immemorial there have been, in
all civilized countries, laws of a restraining
nature, based upon the principle that individuals must curb their propensities, their passions, their desires, whenever, by gratifying
these, the interests of society might be adversely
affected. Robbery, forgery, rape, and arson are
forbidden, because the committal of these crimes,
if permitted, would prove injurious to the welfare of the people in general, though they might
advance the interests of those committing them.

A man is starving; as he drags himself along
the streets, he sees within easy reach the wherewith to satisfy his hunger; but the law stands
between him and the loaf of bread; it warns
him that it were wiser to let his hunger con-
sume him, than to attempt to reduce it by seiz-
ing the loaf. In enforcing this regulation, the
state considers that it is benefiting the community. It is for their welfare—the welfare of
the many as opposed to that of the individual
—that this particular subject must restrain his
desire, his hunger. In other words, the first
law of nature—that of personal self-preservation
—is made subordinate to the code of laws which

was adopted for the preservation of society. The man who is starving cannot steal a loaf of bread to preserve his life, because stealing is destructive to society. The principle is clearly established and recognized that individual interests—no matter how pressing—should not, in any case, supersede general interests. And yet, how limited, in our day, is the application of this excellent principle of restriction. The law which prohibits the gratification of the poor man's hunger at the expense of his neighbor, should, to be logical, prohibit the gratification of the rich man's greed at the expense of his neighbors. If it is just and politic that individuals should be restrained whenever their actions tend to affect adversely the morals and welfare of the community, certainly a check should be imposed on those who, by accumulating wealth far beyond their needs, are instrumental in producing poverty and the crimes and vices which poverty engenders. If personal self-preservation, or self-gratification, must make way for social preservation, then it should be required that the opulent surrender a portion of their riches to save the social organization. If the principle of subjection to restrictions for the general good is one whose application is essential to the welfare of society, then the doctrine of limiting incomes should be recognized, and it should be embodied in laws under the same head as those which compel men to forego, under penalty, certain inclinations, and the indulgence of such passions as might inflict injury on others.

*   *   *   *   *

The Mussulman, true disciple of Mohammed, considers a plurality of wives a luxury; but the extent to which he may indulge this luxury is necessarily regulated by the extent of his wealth. If very rich, he has a harem; if in moderate circumstances, he has one wife; if poor, he has none. Great wealth, therefore, gives him privileges which, it must be admitted, are a serious menace to the general welfare; since a few men of large means might attract to their sides, as wives or odalisques, all the fair maidens in the land. What, then, would be the fate of those who, living in the same country, under the same rule, were unable to procure wives? What, under such conditions—surfeit on one side, want on the other—would become of morals, of society, of the state itself? Let the empires of the East, where no god but Allah is worshipped, where no prophet but Mohammed is recognized, answer.

The Christian, who deems himself more civil-ized than the Mussulman, is not permitted to practice polygamy. Why so? Certainly not from lack of love of luxury; and perhaps not from lack of an inclination towards polygamy. Many reasons are advanced. Some refer, not irrelevantly, to the effect it would have on in-heritance and division of property; but the most plausible reason is that the sexes, being nearly evenly divided, the inevitable result of some men securing a plurality of women, would be to deprive many of having any. It was, therefore, deemed impolitic to permit a certain class to enjoy a privilege, the nature of which could not fail to prove pernicious to the general welfare.

There are, however, other things needful, other things desirable and enjoyable, in the division of which a less equitable, a less politic, spirit is shown. Indeed it would seem that to compensate for this single limitation, unlimited privileges in other respects were granted the fa-vored of fortune. Restricted in the possession of but one legal wife, they are restricted in little else. The extent to which they may enjoy the advantages of life, is regulated only by the extent of their wealth. There being no limit placed on their wealth, whatever riches can purchase is theirs, though others may be wanting in the essentials of life. Their ambition, allowed full sway, knows no bounds, and their greed is beyond the reach of satiety. Everything facilitates their task; everything tends in their direction. There is a strange power whereby gold is drawn towards gold. The greater the accumulation, the greater the attraction. Thus the quantity keeps on increasing while still increasing the attraction for more to be attracted. There are men, in many countries, who annually add more than a million to their possessions. If the same process of accretion were applied to land, and circumstances permitted its continuance, it is evident that a man, acquiring title to several million acres every year, need only live long enough to become possessed of the earth. Considering the vast holdings of certain individuals, the rapid and enormous increase of their wealth, the strenuous and unobstructed efforts they are making to add constantly thereto, and the resultant power thus obtained, there is no reason why a few men should not combine and hold absolute sway over dominions, rivaling, in dimensions and richness, those of mighty states.

As it is, they constitute a power, a veritable Plutocracy, which, so long as it lasts, renders ridiculous all pretensions to the supremacy of Democracy.

Let it not be thought, however, that the lessons of the past are completely lost to memory. The overthrow of certain mighty kings, the reduction of others to mere figureheads, are not mere romances, without historical meaning, without portent of the future. If the power of princes is subject to limitations, surely that of citizens is not beyond restrictions. The principle which should guide Democracy—the principle on which all just government should be based—of subordinating the individual to the general welfare, of allowing each one the freedom to seek and promote his personal interests, only on condition that they interfere in no way with the interests of others, requires, and will obtain, a broader application than at present. Restricting the prerogatives of rulers, and the privileges of nobles and clergy, is not sufficient. Distributing votes and concentrating wealth will not fulfil public aspirations. Prohibiting personal hunger to satisfy itself at the expense of public morality, while allowing personal greed to satisfy itself at the expense of

ıı

the public welfare, does not meet the requirements of equity. Limiting a man to the possession of one wife and according him unlimited
possession of all else, is, assuredly, but a feeble,
and far from successful, attempt to secure a fair
division in the many things subject to division.

No one can doubt that if, in one of the great
modern republics, a few citizens were granted
the privilege of having as many wives as they
chose to gather under their roof, it would be
decried, not only as undemocratic, but as an
excess of luxury derived from semi-barbarous
nations. But it is not considered undemocratic,
in certain quarters, to allow a few citizens the
privilege of accumulating untold millions, and
indulging in the excess of luxury which these
afford. Yet the injustice of this unrestricted
privilege is no less palpable, and the results no
less disastrous, than would be those attending
unrestricted polygamy. The latter is prohibited
by law, and thus the inordinate inclinations of
many are somewhat held in check. But why
does restriction end here? Money is, by universal consent and usage, the medium of exchange for all things. The landowner exchanges
his land, or its use, for money; the farmer exchanges his produce, the merchant his wares,

for money; the laborer, the clerk, the employee of every description, exchange their services for money; the writer exchanges his literary efforts, the poet his effusions, the artist, the sculptor, their inspired productions, for money; nothing, from the commonest comfort to the rarest luxury, can be purchased without money; without it, bread cannot be obtained; it is as necessary to existence as is water, as is air; it is, in the fullest sense of the word, an essential of life to whomsoever lives in a civilized community. Yet we see some who have a superabundance of this essential of life; many who have barely sufficient thereof; others who have none.

It is obvious that if there was less superfluity in some quarters, there would be less want in others; and that greater numbers would be brought within the sphere of comfort. Notwithstanding which fact, there is no country—however boastful of its popular institutions, however jealous of its democratic constitutions—which has on its statute books laws providing that money—the essential of life—shall be so distributed as to benefit the greatest possible number. There are no restrictions on its accumulation, nor on that of any property, its equivalent. In one city—in what is termed a *com-*

monwealth—there are a score of men who have between them a thousand million dollars, while a million souls cannot claim a thousand apiece. These score of men enjoy privileges, and wield a power for weal or for woe—political, financial, and social—greater than those of the million souls combined. And this preponderance of privileges and power is allowed them by a government which is supposed to guarantee to all the enjoyment of equal rights, the enjoyment of equal opportunities.

Call this state of things what you will, but call it not Democracy; claim for it what advantages you please, but claim not that it is advantageous to the nation at large; defend it on whatever grounds you choose, but defend it not on the ground of equity, of morality, or of expediency.

If we reflect well, there is nothing more necessary to prevent the individual interest from subordinating the general interest; there is nothing more essential to secure a fairer distribution of the prizes of life; there is nothing more indispensable to promote the public welfare, to meet the demands of the times, and give consistency to popular government, than regulating the distribution of wealth, and providing against its accumulation in the hands of the few. In no other way can an equilibrium, guaranteeing stability, be established; in no other way can the irrational extremes, immoderate extravagance on one side and absolute want on the other—two evils long deplored, too long tolerated—be obviated; in no other way can the vices to which are traceable the decline of progress and the degeneracy of nations be subdued; in no other way can the area of prosperity expand and thus welcome a larger body of participants; in no other way can the advancement, the improvement, moral and physical, of the people, be accomplished, and the triumph of Democracy achieved.

CHAPTER XII.

CONCLUSION.

IT is not the subversion of the existing system, but the elimination of the abuses and
defects which render it vulnerable and threaten
its continuance, which enlightened Democracy
should advocate. There should be no attempt
to attack or diminish the legitimate authority
of government, but an attempt should be made
to point out its inconsistencies and to bring its
spirit into harmony with its form. It is not
private ownership of property, but its accumulation in the hands of the few, to the detriment
of the many, that should be condemned. No
rights of individuals should be opposed save
those ill-conceived ones which are, in fact,
infringements on the rights of others. No
thought should be more distant than that of
assailing the refined, the cultured class. On
the contrary, the aim should be to increase this
class, till the majority of men are refined and
cultured. Lastly, far from exciting the masses

to disregard prevailing codes, it should be maintained that all laws, however unjust, remain laws, and should be respected, till legally repealed. If this be disregarded, anarchy becomes law. In one word, the people, enjoying supremacy in government, and being entitled to the benefits which that supremacy entails, should use the power which is vested in them —and which allows them to frame the constitution under which they are to live—to alter the conditions which unduly favor some and unduly oppress others; they should require that those regulations, by means of which all the advantages of life are transmitted, for all time, to heirs of a certain class, to the exclusion of all other classes, however intelligent and industrious, be amended; they should insist that the scope of inheritance and accumulation be restricted, and that of opportunity expanded. And in doing this, it will be, not a privilege, but a right, they demand; it will be, not for mercy, but for justice, they contend.

Opposition is to be expected. It is natural to resist the withdrawal of privileges long enjoyed. No matter how iniquitous these may be, their possessor will see iniquity only in being deprived thereof. The slave-owner, overlook-

ing the fact that he was robbing human beings
of their freedom, considered himself robbed of
his slaves when these were emancipated. No
tyrant was ever divested of the power he
usurped, without denouncing the act as unjusti-
fiable and tyrannical. And so the man of opulence who, by various means, has amassed a
vast fortune at the expense of others, will protest vehemently against having to surrender a
portion of his riches. He did not raise his .
voice against the nefarious methods which enabled him, or his ancestors, to despoil the community with impunity; but he will proclaim as
unjust the laws which compel restitution; he
will lament the degeneracy of the age, and
deplore as inhuman the action which, though all
humanity benefit thereby, restrains his grasping
propensities, and cries halt to a selfish ambition
which recognizes no limits.

Since times and conditions are changed; since
ignorance—which, in the past, accounted for the
lowly position of the mass of men—is rapidly
disappearing; since mental superiority—which,
in the early development of society, justified
the elevation of the few over the many—is no
longer the exclusive boast of a small circle,

but the shining distinction of ever-increasing numbers, by what grace of God, by what right, human or divine, do you, O Favorite of Fortune, lay claim to the Sovereignty of this Earth? What becomes of your once recognized privilege to lord it over mankind? What remains of the foundation on which rested the titles to the rich estates you occupy? You refer to ancient law and ancient custom; but remember there is no law, no custom, which is not of man's making, and is not subject to man's unmaking. You point to the sacredness of inheritance; but others will point to its abuses, and ask whether your claims in this respect are more valid than those of certain kings—of Charles of England, of Louis of France—whose exalted pretensions saved neither their thrones nor their heads. You demand the reward of superior genius; but you demand it at the expense of a host of victims, as did the victorious warrior who, on the ruins of fallen monarchy, built a mighty empire and, laughing at inheritance, proclaimed himself a modern Cæsar. Forget not, however, that his vast dominions, conquered and ruled by his dazzling genius, were wrested from his control; that his imperial

crown, the most resplendent the world had
seen, was exchanged, against his will, for that
of a Mediterranean islet; and that, as you
will, he rebelled against the substitution of
the smaller for the greater realm.   He who had
ruled over France disdained to rule over the
petty island kingdom; he sighed to reconquer
the glories of the past; to breathe once more
the entrancing atmosphere of yore.   He sailed,
on the ship of Destiny, from Elba to Waterloo;
from Waterloo to St. Helena.   There, alas!
no crown awaited him; no sceptre; no dominion,
however small.   The sun of Empire had set;
the last shadow of grandeur had vanished.   The
ambition which knew no limit, the spirit which
panted for universal conquest, was confined
to a solitary rock in the stormy wastes of the
Atlantic.

Thus ended the career of one who aspired
to the sovereignty of the earth.

Do you, O Money-king, claim a genius more
commanding, an influence more weighty, than
that of the haughty conqueror of Europe, who
had proud princes for courtiers, rich kingdoms
for provinces?   Face to face with the superior
forces, the paramount rights, of others, to what

star will you turn, to what power will you appeal, for exemption from a fate which attended the greatest of mortals?

Pause and reflect.

The choice is yours: Elba or St. Helena?

THE END